STAR CRUISE: MAROONED

VERONICA SCOTT

To my daughters Valerie and Elizabeth, and my brother David for all his encouragement and support through the years. He'd be a great guy to have along in any survival situation!

ACKNOWLEDGMENT

Julie C and The E-book Formatting Fairies!

CHAPTER ONE

The shuttle broke out of the cloud layer and swooped over a breathtaking vista of pink and green foliage, practically glowing in the vid screens. The rainforest spread across the planet as far as the scanners could detect. Clouds of multicolored birds flew above the treetops, drawing the eye to their wheeling movement across the turquoise sky. Here and there, rainbows curved from puffy clouds, where seasonal showers had added moisture to the air. As Meg walked through the cabin, offering refreshments to their guests, she attempted to direct their attention to the view of the planet. Anchored by trees soaring hundreds of feet from the surface, the foliage and avian wildlife were something never seen on the highly civilized worlds where these people lived and worked. Although they'd paid a staggering amount of credits to be taken to this site, neither the primary guest, nor the people he'd brought, seemed to care. Drinking, playing cards, and indulging in sexual innuendo took all their attention.

Not much changed from cruise to cruise with the rich and powerful, despite Meg's best efforts to share the simple pleasure she found in the surroundings at each port of call.

At the rear of the main cabin, she found at least one passenger watching the screen above her seat. "How are you doing?"

Callina Finchon Bettis took her attention from the view for a moment, giving Meg a little wave. "Fine, smooth ride so far. When can we see the Falls?"

"Soon. The pilot likes to swoop in from the front, as if we're going to splash right through the water." Meg leaned closer. "But don't worry, he veers to the side at the last moment." She placed an iced fruit drink at the woman's elbow. "Maybe five more minutes."

As Callina murmured thanks, Meg retreated to the galley, where she found the only other crew member besides the pilot.

"Passengers all happy now?" he asked, raising one eyebrow.

"I don't think this bunch is ever happy," she said. "You'll find generational billionaires rarely are, when you've done more of these private charters. But at least I've supplied them with feelgoods." She slid the drink tray into the chiller. "Did you need something?"

Simon 'Red' Thomsill held up his hands in mock surrender. "I know, this is your territory and I shouldn't be here, Guild rules. But the pilot wanted coffee."

Hands on her hips, Meg smothered an impatient sigh. "First of all, he should have buzzed me for it, and secondly, he knows perfectly well only guests are entitled to genuine Terran coffee."

"Wow, are you this dedicated to rules all the time?" He leaned against the emergency portal and studied her, one eyebrow raised as if he might be trying to tease her.

Two internal call signals pinged, one right after the other. From the cabin, she heard female passengers swearing at each other. She straightened her tunic as if gathering determination, and headed out to mediate whatever the problem was now. "No tip is going to be big enough," she said under her breath. Pausing on the threshold, she glanced at Red. "I'm responsible for the coffee inventory on this shuttle, and it comes out of my pay if the weight is short."

"I didn't know."

"Yeah, there's a lot you don't know, rookie. But Drewson does. The synth stuff crew members drink is over there." Pointing at the proper carafe, she left the galley as more voices joined the clamor in the passenger section.

One of the scantily clad women had spilled her beverage all over another's ample cleavage, staining both the woman's skin and skimpy bikini top. The agressor was pulling the other's hair and screaming insults, while her victim tried to land some blows anywhere she could reach. The primary guest laughed and made bets with the two men seated next to him, wagering on which woman would prevail.

Meg waded into the fray. "Ladies, please, we're about to land. You're required to be in your seats before we can make our final approach." She caught the second woman's elbow. Modulating her voice to a soothing tone, Meg said, "I can remove the stain, Ma'am, no problem."

The women paused in their altercation, gazing beyond her with wide eyes. A moment later, both fluffed their hair.

Without turning, Meg knew Red had followed her. She'd observed his effect on females more than once already on this cruise. Something about his 6'4" height, the heavily muscled biceps, the chiseled features, the sparkling green eyes…Well, okay, to be honest, he had the same effect on her, but she wasn't about to let him know. Been there, done that with a tempting crewman or two on her early tours. Crew romances were nothing but trouble when the first attraction inevitably flamed out.

Although Red was more tempting than anyone she'd met in a long time.

"Second Officer Drewson asked me to come and make sure the accommodations and the service are satisfactory," he said, his voice deep and slow.

"Oh, yes, we're fine." The girl with the stained top brushed at her skin, accentuating her ample chest with the gesture, and smiled as if she hadn't been screeching obscenities a moment prior.

"So nice of you." The other batted her three eyes at Red, green lashes sweeping her cheeks. She held out her arm. "I think I might have a scratch."

"I'll get the medkit while Miss Antille helps Sharmali," he said, leaning close to inspect the tiny red mark on the passenger's creamy skin.

"Fine." Meg was pissed and she planned to let him know it. What the seven hells did he think he was doing, interfering with her care for her passengers? He was crew, not service. She wasn't the rookie here. Following Sharmali to her seat, Meg drew the cleaning pod from her belt and passed it a few inches above the woman's skin and the orange and purple fabric of the bikini top. The pod hummed and the stains lifted in a rain of reverse droplets, absorbed into the cleaner, leaving no trace.

Not bothering with thanks, Sharmali practically shoved Meg out of the way to return to where Red was patting soothing ointment on the second passenger's face, having already bandaged the red mark on her arm. Moving past the seat where the first aid was occurring, Meg rolled her eyes. The mark was so tiny, it didn't merit discussing, much less treatment. Or his holding the woman's hand as she hyperventilated.

Irritation at the cozy scene flooded Meg's nerves, making her voice a bit on the shrill side. "Don't you have to return to the flight deck, Officer Thomsill?" Technically, she outranked him when it came to passenger care.

He gave her an enigmatic look, gathered the medical supplies, and headed for the galley behind her. "You're welcome," he said as she keyed the privacy screen between them and the passenger seats.

"Listen, I didn't ask for your help and I don't need it. You made me appear incompetent just now." Grabbing the medkit from him, she stuffed it into the proper niche, slamming the compartment door.

Eyebrows raised, he rocked back on his heels. "That wasn't my intention."

"We'll be landing in three minutes, folks." Drewson's voice on the com was authoritative. "The Falls is coming into range on your vidscreens. Officer Thomsill, you're needed on the flight deck."

"Saved by the pilot, or I'd be giving you a piece of my mind," Meg said, shaking her finger at Red. "Don't forget his synth coffee."

Red reached past her to grab the carafe. Leaning close, invading her personal space, he said, "We'll continue this conversation later."

As he ascended in the one level gravlift to rejoin the pilot, she took a deep breath, pasted on her professional expression, and returned to the cabin to ensure the passengers were seated for landing and could perhaps be cajoled to spare a moment to glimpse the extremely expensive view.

"Took you long enough," Drewson said as Red reached the cockpit.

"Here's your synth," he answered, more than a little annoyed. He suspected Drewson had set him up.

The pilot guffawed as he accepted the steaming drink. "Miss By-The-Book wouldn't give you the real stuff, would she? Didn't think she would."

Red sank into his chair, rubbing the back of his neck. Yeah, his trip to the cabin had sure gone well. He'd managed to annoy Meg twice in ten minutes. Third time and he'd be a total write-off as far as she was concerned. Good intentions didn't get him too far. *Need to up your game, Thomsill.* Meg was the only reason he'd signed on to this outfit. One glance at her, sitting at the next table in the Guild canteen on Sector Hub and he'd been a goner. Something about her sweet face and sparkling hazel eyes stuck in a man's memory.

When he heard there was an opening on this ship for a Third Officer, he'd put his other opportunity on hold, entered his bid, and apparently the captain liked his experience. But this was next to the last stop on the charter and so far Meg barely gave him the time of day. If she spoke to him at all. The other officers and crew members said she kept to herself and never dated co-workers. Which was smart of her, but didn't help him much. The Sectors was a galaxy-wide civilization, the cushy job on hold for him with the CLC Line wouldn't wait forever, and he might never see her again if he let this opportunity fall through.

He'd never had much of a problem getting to know a woman before. Of course, none of them had mattered to him as much as Meg did. Desire to impress her made him self-conscious and fall over his own big feet.

Every time.

"Told you she's impossible," Drewson said. "I tried on our first cruise together, but she shut me down hard."

"Well quit 'helping' me, okay? I can screw this up enough on my own." Red hid his frustration under a light tone.

"Gonna miss you, rookie, if you don't sign on with us again. It's been a treat watching you try to make an impression on Meg. You should have gone after the Chief Stewardess. She's been eyeing you, in case you haven't gotten the message."

Except he wasn't the least bit interested in anyone but Meg. Red gave himself a mental shake. He could plan complex operations in the field, improvise on the fly under the worst conditions, and had the medals to prove it—why couldn't he manage to establish some kind of less than antagonistic relationship with Meg Antille? See if there was any potential for something between them? Not for the first time, he berated himself for being an idiot, following a woman he'd only barely met across the Sector…but somehow a chance with Meg seemed worth it.

Drewson fiddled with the controls. "Check the atmospherics, would you? Make sure those storms are tracking out to sea."

"Yes, sir." Glad to be distracted, even for a moment, Red gave his attention to the instruments.

True to Meg's prediction, Drewson took the shuttle in through the iridescent spray thrown off by the Rainbow Falls, and executed a smooth landing on the small landing pad next to the beach. As she triggered the door to allow the passengers to exit for their excursion today, Meg said, "We'll be here for four hours, so you have plenty of time to stroll along the beach, enjoy the view, and relax. It's safe to swim in the lake, but please, no further out than the marker buoys where the sonic barrier begins. The crew and I'll be setting up your pavilion and amenities, and serving the requested lunch in about an hour."

The music the Falls was famed for thundered outside. The water was effervescent, filled with bubbles of all the colors of the rainbow, having leached minerals from the planet's surface as the river flowed toward the solitary ocean. The way the liquid poured through the cliff's rocky channels and crevices produced constantly changing crystalline "music." Meg loved it here. Dantaralon was one of her favorite spots. She stepped outside for a moment herself, before the work had to begin again. The air was warm, redolent with scent from the many flowering plants.

"Wow." Red descended the short ramp to stand beside her, staring at the waterfall in the distance. "Impressive, like the brochures promised."

"We specialize in conveying our passengers on a tour of exotic natural wonders," Meg said. "This part of Sector Thirty is full of amazing sights on so many planets."

"Seen one waterfall, seen them all. Come on, let's get this done before the Primary starts complaining." Drewson left the shuttle, jumped off the ramp, and went to open the cargo hold.

"Mr. Finchon and his guests have the place pretty much to themselves," Red said, eyeing the empty landing pad, which held only one other shuttle, parked at the other end of the grid. "He should appreciate the exclusivity of the situation. Is this place usually so deserted?"

Meg paused to take a second look. Red was right, there was only one set of charter cruise passengers already on the beach. She recognized the TDJ Lines banner flying from their gaudy turquoise pavilion. "Odd, while this isn't peak season, we usually have to share with more neighbors than this."

"Can we cut the chitchat?" Drewson activated the three stubby robos inside the now-open hold. One after the other they trundled down their ramp, moving smoothly onto the terrain on their antigrav. The pilot tossed the control to Meg. "All yours."

She'd done this routine many a time. Directing the robos to the beach was simple. Once there, the biggest unfolded itself into a pavilion similar to TDJ's, if less colorful, and the other two disgorged lounge chairs, her cooking apparatus, and more necessary equipment.

Red brought the food and drink module, parking it next to Meg. "Are you sure you don't need help? Shouldn't the Chief Stew have come along today?"

"Yes, ideally, but she said she had a headache." Meg was busy unwrapping the precooked hors d'oeuvres. "It's only a beach picnic, half the passengers didn't come. I can deal. And she's going to work ahead on décor for dinner, consult with the chef, all the arrangements the guests will never even notice. Will you go set up the flotation devices and the net for games, in case anyone actually wants to play?"

"Aye aye." He gave her a mock salute and trotted closer to the lakeshore, where the guests were settling into their comfortable chairs.

Meg followed to take drinks orders. The next hour or so was busy, but she enjoyed the pace. Made the time pass.

Moments before she was ready to serve lunch, Red checked in with her again.

"Anything else you need?"

She realized her party hadn't cleared their presence yet with the park rangers. Pushing her bangs off her forehead, she said, "Yes, can you do me a favor and run to the ranger station on the far side of the landing field? Usually, someone would have come by to check our permit, but maybe there's a staff meeting running long or something. Tell the person at the desk our permits are in order, and I can show them after I've served lunch. Our line has a good reputation, so the ranger should be okay about it."

"No problem." Despite his cheerful answer, he hesitated. "What does Drewson do on these trips ashore?"

"As little as possible, believe me. Privilege of rank, or so he says. Actually, he's not too good with the guests, so his absence is probably better for all of us, as far as the size of the tip at the end of the voyage." Meg hoped she hadn't said too much to the rookie, but her frustrations with Drewson grew every time he was assigned as the pilot bringing her ashore with passengers.

As Red walked away, she served the buffet luncheon, which met with approval from their guests. The *Far Horizon* featured one of the Virochol Lines' most experienced gourmet chefs—he shipped out as a package deal with their Captain, so her ship was much sought after for charters.

Red came to report in the middle of lunch service, a puzzled frown on his face.

"What did the ranger say?" Meg asked, plating more mini sandwiches.

Shaking his head, Red said, "No one there."

"What?" She paused in the middle of drizzling artful condiments on the individual Azrigone beef patties. Laughing, thinking perhaps he was kidding, she said, "Are they out to lunch or something?"

"Place is all closed up. I knocked, on the off chance someone was left as a caretaker, but the station shows all the signs of being abandoned." He ran one hand through the dark maroon hair that gave him his nickname.

"Impossible. The rangers and their families live here year round. I'll go check for myself later." Annoyed at his failure to complete the simple task, she said, "Mr. Trever asked to go fishing, and that's your job."

"Any hints on the best spot?" Red surveyed the lake.

"I never paid much attention. I think there's a sand bar off to the left. Try there." She gestured vaguely. "The fishing gear is in the boat module, which you'll have to bring from the shuttle."

Red departed to handle the task and she kept serving lunch and drinks. A few minutes later, she heard the purr of the small boat's motor and raised her head long enough to watch Red skippering three guests onto the beautifully colored lake.

Finishing the lunch service, she had a bit of free time before the mid afternoon snack. Mingling with the passengers held no appeal for her. She wasn't working charters to try and snag a generational billionaire or intergalactic businessman.

Meg sent as many of her credits as she could to her family, on their home world, to buy more land for the Antille spice farms. Scanning the beach for a moment, she considered the primary guest and the men he'd brought along on this cruise. A mix of businessmen like himself and faded celebrities to fawn over him and impress the men he wanted to do deals with. Shaking her head, she couldn't wait to see the last of this bunch.

Taking a glass of the refreshing faquilada fruit drink, she wandered toward the TDJ pavilion, hoping she knew a few of the cruise staff or crew. A woman in the other line's uniform came to meet her, waving cordially. Delighted, Meg recognized Sallira, a casual acquaintance in the Guild. Their circle of mutual friends was wide, so catching up on gossip took a few minutes. Then Meg said, "Hey, what's the deal with the ranger station? My guy said it was closed. Did you see anyone official when you landed?"

Sallira shook her head. "No, he's right, the staff is all gone." Making a funny face of regret, lips scrunched, she sighed. "Too bad, I had a flirtation going with the senior ranger last time I was here." One eyebrow raised suggestively, she sipped her drink. "I was anticipating more fun and games this trip, if you know what I mean." She nudged Meg in the ribs with her elbow. "Harmless fun, but he sure was cute."

Meg stared at the Falls and then the lake. The park gave the appearance of order, serene and beautiful as always. Maybe the Sector Thirty government had decided to cut costs by eliminating the rangers? But then why hadn't she seen a bulletin to that effect? The captain gave her the permit token before the shuttle left the *Far Horizon* this morning, so he must not have known the permanent staff was gone either.

There was a shout from the TDJ pavilion. One of the crew was hustling their obviously bewildered passengers toward Meg and Sallira, while a second man ran ahead, sprinting for the landing field as if he had a major predator on his heels. The other cruise staff member was matching him stride for stride, but skidded to a stop in the sand next to Sallira, breathing hard. "We gotta go, right now."

Eyes wide, the woman's jaw dropped. "What are you talking about?"

"Captain called, emergency channel, said get our butts up to the ship immediately."

Sallira twisted her hair into a knot as she prepared to return to work. "I guess gossip time is over, sorry, Meg. I'll go pack the gear—"

But the other TDJ woman was shaking her head, pulling her by the elbow. "No, the captain said leave everything. Run before the pilot leaves *us*."

"Is there something I should know?" Meg asked. No one ever abandoned the expensive robots and gear. Unease stirred in her gut.

"I don't know, captain didn't give any details. We're out of here." The staffer grabbed a dawdling child who was digging a hole in the sand, and hurried to the incline leading to the shuttles.

"Guess I better go," Sallira said. "Maybe you should check with your captain, might be a solar flare or something."

Her crewmates were yelling and gesturing for Sallira to hurry so she didn't linger for any more chitchat, taking off at a fast pace, leaving Meg alone on the beach. Moments later, the TDJ shuttle lifted straight from the pad and shot into the azure sky. Meg rubbed her elbow, suddenly feeling goose bumps. The beach wasn't as welcoming anymore, despite the bright sun and the ethereal music from the Falls. The forlorn pavilion and humming equipment bothered her.

"What's with them?"

She jumped, turning to find Red standing behind her. This time it was a bit comforting to have him by her side. "I don't know."

"Is the other crew coming back later for their stuff?" His face was set in serious lines.

"I-I don't know." Meg walked toward their own set up. "The TDJ staff member in charge said their captain got on the com from orbit about some emergency and recalled them."

"Did we get any bulletins?" Red asked. "Storms? Warn offs?"

She shook her head. "Not that I heard of. You're ship's crew, you're more likely to know than I am. Think I should ask Drewson to check in with the *Far Horizon?*"

He scanned the beach, eyes hooded. "Yeah, I think you've got a good idea. I'll cover things here."

Meg handed him her empty glass. "Do you mind turning off their power grid?"

Eyebrows raised, he gave her an incredulous stare. "The TDJ staff left the equipment running?"

Not bothering to answer beyond a distracted nod, she made her way to the landing pad. The shuttle portal was locked, which seemed like excessive caution on Drewson's part, but of course she had the override code. The cabin was empty, but she heard sounds from the rear, where there was a luxurious private bedroom. Reluctantly, she walked aft. Drewson and at least one of the passengers were obviously enjoying themselves, from the exclamations and noises she was overhearing. Maybe he wasn't as bad with interpersonal relations as she'd believed.

She knocked on the thick Zulairian mahogany door, another of the many expensive touches on their shuttle. Luxury all the way, was the Virochol Lines' boast.

No answer, but the voices inside the room had gone silent.

She rapped her knuckles on the door again. "Drewson, it's Meg. I need to talk to you—we may have a problem."

The door opened a crack, enough for her to see her fellow crew member's naked body. Averting her eyes, she said, "Have you heard anything from the ship?"

"Of course not. Why would I?" Drewson's smile was more of a leer. "I've been busy."

"There's something weird going on—"

"I'm waiting," said an impatient female voice from further inside the room. "You don't want me to get cold, do you?"

The Second Officer turned his head a fraction. "I'll warm you up again, baby, no problem."

Meg tamped down her irritation. He was risking his job, not to mention the tip the entire crew worked for, if he got caught screwing a guest while on duty, but he was her commanding officer right now. He could make a lot of trouble for her. She wasn't going to yield on her demand, though. "I think we need to check with the ship."

"All *right*," he said, a rough edge of anger in his voice. He shut the door in her face and opened it open a moment later, extending his hand, the control panel token dangling on the chain of his suskadi-foot lucky charm. "You know how to open the coms; you call if you're so damn worried. Tell them I'm attending to passenger relations, understand? And barring war breaking out between the rangers and us, do *not* interrupt me a second time." The threat was clear.

"Yes, sir."

The door slammed in her face. Meg turned and walked slowly to the bow, where the gravlift to the cockpit was located. Doubt assailed her. There were bound to be awkward questions why she was calling the ship. Maybe the TDJ crew had a problem with their vessel, nothing at all to do with anything affecting their own situation. In the galley, she paused, swinging the little good luck charm. "Am I overreacting?" Red didn't think so, but then he was a rookie. Although rumor had it he was retired military, Special Forces or something, a drifter now, bumming his way through the galaxy pleasure spots. Maybe his opinion did count more than most rookie crew members'. Chewing her lip, she sank into her jump seat. But the passengers were her responsibility right now and the TDJ crew had abandoned a lot of pricey hardware in their haste to leave.

"Okay, I'll pretend I need clarification on dinner tonight, something the Primary might have asked." Plan in mind, she left the chair to take the gravlift into the cockpit.

All kinds of lights were flashing and there was a loud klaxon sounding. Hands over her ears, Meg rushed to the com panel, which she'd received cursory cross-training on, early in her stint as a cruise staff member. Hesitating for a moment, she flipped the controls to off. Then she swallowed hard and opened the link to their ship in stationary orbit above.

"Hello, *Far Horizon*, shuttle calling—"

"Where the seven hells have you been? Where's Drewson?" The voice she heard was so strained she could barely recognize the First Officer.

She drew breath to speak, but was cut off.

"Never mind, tell him everything's—"

There was a funny sort of crackle from the link and then silence. She waited a few moments, then tried closing and reopening the connection. Nothing. Ship to space atmospherics could be a chancy thing. Drewson had made it clear he would *not* appreciate her interrupting his private party twice, and anyway, right now there was no talking to the ship.

The panel indicated someone else had entered the shuttle. Callina's voice came over the internal com. "Meg? Are you here?"

She flipped the switch. "I'm in the cockpit. What do you need?" The last thing she wanted was the woman going near the private bedroom.

"Mr. Thomsill sent me to get you and the medkit. Sharmali's been bitten by some kind of eel thing and she's bleeding really bad."

"I'll be right down." Meg rose, staring at the now quiet com board. She decided to leave the ship-to-ship and general hailing frequencies open. With mischievous amusement, she piped the links directly to the luxury cabin, set at high volume. If the ship did call again, Drewson was going to know it. He could make his own excuses when he answered. She could always claim she'd forgotten how to adjust the volume.

When the gravlift deposited her in the galley, Callina was waiting, shifting from foot to foot, tears on her cheeks. Rushing to tell her news, the passenger's words tumbled out. "Sharmali was in the water and this thing grabbed her, pulled her under. Mr. Thomsill rescued her. I've never seen anything like it, outside the adventure trideos. He was amazing, the way he fought the beast in the water with his knife. But she's screaming and there's so much blood."

"He didn't get bitten too, did he?"

Callina shook her head. "I don't think so. He was acting normal."

Deciding at most Sharmali had fallen afoul of a non-venomous water snake, because the sonic barrier kept the serious predators at bay, Meg grabbed the medkit and handed it to Callina. More of the female passenger's drama over nothing. "Here, there should be all the equipment and medicines he needs to treat Sharmali's bite. I'm sure the wound can't be too bad. Tell him I'll be right there."

Sniffling, Callina sprinted for the exit. Meg looked around, anxiety making her queasy. Where was she going to leave the precious control panel token? Of course Drewson could operate the shuttle without it—there was a backup hidden where only he knew—but he'd be angry if she kept it. Guild rules and all. Deciding to stash it in his coffee mug, she stepped to the left when something caught her eye—an unmarked, sealed compartment where the officers' weapons were held. Did she dare? Yes, today she did. Things were definitely going awry and getting scarier. Drewson could give her hell later, but if one of the deadly eels had somehow gotten inside the barrier on the beach, other predatory creatures might be in the vicinity as well. Her passengers could be in jeopardy.

It took only a moment to unlock the panel with Drewson's token, and withdraw the two small blasters. After resealing the cabinet, she stuck the weapons in a bag meant for cleaning supplies, threw the token into Drewson's coffee mug as planned, and ran from the shuttle. The door sealed shut after her.

On the beach, there was chaos. An eel, easily two feet in diameter and eight feet long, lay convulsing on the sand, Red's hunting knife buried to the hilt in one eye. The crewman had the medkit open beside him and was struggling to staunch the blood flow from Sharmali's lower leg, while she lay on a red-stained towel and moaned. Callina was standing beside them, trying to help. The other men and women milled on the beach nearby, drinking and talking in too loud voices. As Meg headed for the injured passenger, the Primary intercepted her.

"Miss Antille, I demand to know how something like this could happen." Purple in the face, he waved a hand at Sharmali. "I paid top dollar, if not an exorbitant price, for a safe, enjoyable cruise for myself and my guests, and now the poor girl's had her foot eaten!" He was so upset he was spitting.

"On behalf of the Line, I certainly apologize, sir. We do everything we can to ensure the safety of our guests under all circumstances, but if she swam beyond the sonic barrier—"

"She was standing in three inches of water right next to me," Finchon said. "That monster could have just as easily gotten my foot."

"The barrier's off," Red informed her, not glancing up from his task. "Can you argue with him later? I need your help."

Meg ran to his side, the Primary matching her step for step, yelling at her about lawsuits and refunds. She tried to stem the tide of his vitriol so she could concentrate. "Sir, please, let us assist Sharmali, and then I'll be happy to discuss the legalities."

Trever, the retired pro athlete, came forward and took his host by the arm, shoving a drink into his hand and drawing him aside. Meg took a deep breath of relief and knelt beside Red. "What do you want me to do?"

"Apply pressure to the wound for a minute while I see what antivenom we've got."

Gulping against her nausea, Meg set her hand on the makeshift bandages and pressed hard. "You said the barrier was off?"

"Must be. There was more than one of these things right in the shallows at the beach. We were lucky no one else got attacked. I got her out of the water as fast as I could so the blood wouldn't attract other predators." He sat on his heels, frowning, holding an inject. "This is only a generic. Will it work on eel venom?"

"It's all we've got on the shuttle. It'll have to hold her until we get to the ship's sick bay."

As he gave Sharmali the inject, Meg eyed the wound with deep misgiving. The woman's leg was definitely swelling and there were ugly purple streaks advancing toward her knee. "This is my fault," she said.

"How do you figure?" Red applied a light tourniquet.

"I should have known if the ranger station was closed, the barriers might be shut off, but I didn't check."

"Well, keep your voice down, the Primary is pissed off enough right now. Don't add fuel to his fire. We'd better get her to the shuttle and hustle offplanet, to the ship. What did you find out?" He turned to take more towels from Callina with a murmured thanks and wrapped the oversize, gaily colored fabric around Sharmali. "She's going into shock, gotta keep her warm."

"Drewson said he hadn't heard anything. I called the ship myself, but we got interrupted. Signal failed or something." Meg rose as he did, admiring the smooth manner in which Red lifted the injured woman, not jostling her.

"We'll know soon enough." He shifted Sharmali to lie more comfortably against his chest and walked away as if her weight was nothing to him. "Guess it's our turn to leave the equipment behind, at least temporarily."

"Oh, Lords of Space, of course." Meg grabbed the cleaning supplies bag, since the blasters were in there, thankfully unneeded. She detoured to flip the switch turning off the power grid, dropped the bag inside the nearest robo's storage cavity to leave her hands free, and then caught up to the guests at the base of the walkway leading to the landing pad.

The rumble of the shuttle's engines caught her by surprise. How could Drewson possibly know about the emergency? As she decided he must have checked the beach-facing vidscreens for some reason, the tenor of the sound changed from warmup to full power. In disbelief, she saw the shuttle rising from the pad.

"What the seven hells is he doing?" Red yelled.

"Stay clear, don't get caught in the backflare," Meg screamed, pulling at the guests. Most shrank away from the landing pad, but the Primary strode up the ramp, shaking his fist and yelling curses at the pilot. Red set Sharmali in the sand and sprinted to tackle Finchon before he got crisped. The two men rolled on the ramp, the ungrateful host trying to punch Red.

As the crewman laid their passenger out with a swift right hook to the jaw, the shuttle cleared the trees and shot into the sky, leaving them behind in the blink of an eye.

"Now what?" Callina said, shielding her eyes with one hand as she watched the shuttle grow smaller and smaller in the sky. "He won't forget to pick us up later will he?"

"Of course he won't," Meg said, fear making it hard to enunciate. The captain would send Drewson or someone to collect them. He wouldn't abandon half his passengers and two of his crew, would he?

"What do we do now?" asked one of the female passengers in a shaky voice.

Realizing the entire group was all watching her with varying degrees of puzzlement, fear, and annoyance, Meg cleared her throat. "I think Mr. Thomsill and I need to see if we can get the ranger station open. Sharmali would be better off there while we wait for the shuttle to return, than lying on the open beach. But if you'd like to resume your picnic, there's no reason not to. We're scheduled to be here for two more hours. I'm sure the crew'll come pick us up on time."

"Where are Lindy and Sam?" someone asked, voice rising in alarm.

"And Pirankai?" said Trever, scanning the faces around him, forehead wrinkled in a frown.

"Pirankai was on the shuttle, um conferring with Mr. Drewson," Meg answered, rapidly, remembering that the retired athlete had been quite cozy with the lithe blond passenger for the last day or so. She hoped he didn't put two and two together about what Drewson and Pirankai might have been doing, or the entire crew's tip might be diminished. Counting heads, all worries over the eventual tip fled as she realized she'd failed in yet another duty. Two of her passengers were missing and would have been left behind temporarily if the rest had gone in the shuttle with Drewson. "We'll have to find them," she said. "Does anyone remember what direction Lindy and Sam went?"

"Right now, we have other priorities," Red interrupted. "The two of them'll probably come wandering in of their own volition soon enough. I'm sure if we searched we'd find them, uh, admiring the scenery someplace close by, which would be embarrassing for everyone concerned. Okay, folks, I think Miss Antilles had an excellent idea—you might as well relax, and follow the original plan for now."

"Can I get two volunteers to help us get Sharmali settled at the ranger station?" Meg asked. "Keep an eye on her?"

"Well, don't look at me," Harelly said, as several of the other guests glanced in his direction. "I only *play* a doctor on the trideo shows. The sight of blood makes me ill."

Callina and her husband, Peter, volunteered. As the other passengers slowly hiked through the sand to their pavilion by the lake, Meg, Red, and the volunteers headed for the ranger station on the far side of the landing pad.

"What about him?" asked Bettis, who Meg remembered was Finchon's employee, a personal assistant or something. He and his wife filed past the groggy charter Primary, who was sitting now, holding his jaw.

"I'll deal with him later," Red said.

"He's gonna be pissed. He's gonna sue you and your company for every credit," the man predicted, excitement in his voice. "He'll probably end up owning the whole cruise line before he's done."

"Not my problem right now." Red's voice was cheerful.

Meg admired his attitude. She was dizzy with anxiety and worry, happy to follow his lead for the moment. What in the seven hells had Drewson been thinking, taking off without them?

The ranger station was ominously quiet. The storm shutters were latched and the usually immaculate landscaping had become overgrown, weeds running riot, untrimmed vines establishing a foothold on the ornamental fence, and even scaling one wall.

"How long do you guess the rangers have been gone?" Meg said, eyeing the building. She glanced at the living quarters to the left, noticing the same general run down air. The three small houses were tightly sealed, as if hunched against a coming storm.

"The forest grows fast," Red said. "Probably not more than a few months. I wonder why we weren't warned, though."

"Warned?" Callina Bettis picked up on his remark. "Are we in some kind of danger?"

Red and Meg exchanged glances. "He means we should have been notified there wouldn't be any immediate help onsite," Meg said, forcing herself to speak the lie calmly. "In case of an emergency, like the unfortunate bite Sharmali suffered."

Setting the injured woman on a picnic table, Red went to the front door of the station, Meg on his heels. She tried activating the portal to no avail, punching the tabs hard. "You think the last person out would have left it set to open, general access, in case anyone needed help the way we do." She thumped her fist on the door.

"Unless the staff didn't expect anyone to be here," Red said. "Are you sure there's not something you forgot to tell me?"

"I swear, you know as much as I do." She leaned closer and lowered her voice. "Drewson was boning Pirankai in the private cabin when I got to the shuttle, coms off, so if there were any bulletins, he missed them."

"Idiot." Red retreated a step or two, eyeing the door. "Well, nothing for it."

"Are you going to break it down?"

Eyebrows raised, he gave her a glance. "Thanks for the compliment but it'd take a battle robo to get through this storm portal by brute force."

"What then?"

He stepped to the keypad, flipping open the cover, and entered a series of numbers and symbols so rapidly she had no idea what the sequence might be.

"You've been here before?" Meg asked.

He shook his head. "Special Forces, Team Twelve. We each have a special access code enabling our entry into any door, ship, vault, or facility in the Sectors."

The storm door jerked away from the threshold and then began to roll into the roof recess. The window shutters on all four sides of the building followed suit a moment later. Meg knew her mouth was hanging open. Biting her lip, she tried to make sense of this new information. "You're on active military duty, but working as crew on a charter ship? Are you undercover or something?"

"Retired. Wasn't sure my code would work, but we have a saying in the Teams—no one is ever completely released from service." He grimaced. "Not until we die or the Mawreg have been erased from the Sectors. I should live so long." He pushed the inner door open. "Let's see what we have here. Stay behind me."

The lights didn't respond to voice command or their physical presence. "I guess the rangers powered down before departing. Shutters must be on auxiliary. I'll have to check the situation out later," he said, pausing on the threshold. "At least the windows let in enough ambient light for now."

"How long do you think we're going to be here?" Meg was disturbed by his mention of later.

"Depends on what the problem in orbit is." He stopped, giving her a hard look. "Anything like this ever happen before?"

"No. Drewson is an idiot, but he'd never abandon us. And Captain Jonsle certainly won't maroon us."

"He may not have a choice. I don't want to alarm you, but we could be in a bad situation here. I hope not, but just between the two of us, I'm not feeling too positive. Whatever spooked the TDJ captain into recalling his people had to be damn serious. I don't want to alarm our passengers because panicked people are hard to handle. Drewson's takeoff seems like the act of a panicked person." He studied her face, the expression on his serious. "You're not going to panic, are you?"

"Of course not." She straightened her spine, irritated he would even ask.

He squeezed her shoulder. "Good. I didn't think so. Stay here, let me check the rest of the place, and then we'll bring Sharmali in."

Moving so quietly she couldn't hear his footsteps, Red left her. Meg sank onto the nearest chair, resting her head in her hands. If she and the people she was responsible for were in survival mode, even for a short time until someone sent help for them, she had to reprioritize her thoughts. By the time Red returned to the small lobby, she was on her feet, pacing, and making lists on her personal AI.

"Nothing left behind but the furniture as far as I can see," Red reported brusquely. There's a big conference room or maybe it's a dining room, and a small kitchen, couple of offices."

"Right. We'll bring Sharmali in here, lay her on the couch. If you can't get the power going, we can build a fire for tonight. The temperatures plummet after dark and the wind rises. There's a fireplace in the conference room too, right?"

He nodded. "Plenty of wood stacked out back. We can do the rustic thing. Maybe the guests will enjoy the novelty of camping out tonight."

"Hope so, as that's their only choice. I think we leave the guests in blissful ignorance for now, until the Primary asks about missing the deadline for retrieval. It'll dawn on them soon enough we're marooned, if we truly are." Meg checked his reaction. "Seem okay to you?"

His calm face betrayed nothing. "Yes, Ma'am. But eventually they're going to get upset. Especially the Primary, Mr. Finchon. He has a short fuse."

"He's not in charge anymore, I am." Meg dropped her AI into a handy pocket. "This is a survival situation and I'm the senior crew member."

She half expected him to protest, but his eyebrows lifted in mock surprise and he agreed with enthusiasm. "Yes, you are. And I'm here to back you to the hilt."

"Hey, what's going on in there?" Bettis, the male passenger, peered into the lobby. "Can we bring Sharmali in or not?"

"Yes, we've got a nice couch to put her on, make her comfortable." Red moved to join him, saying to Meg in a low voice as he passed, "You and I need to talk more, later."

Red arranged Sharmali on the couch, Meg and Callina covering her with the large, soft beach towels. As she tucked the cloth over Sharmali's shoulders, touching her clammy skin, Meg was alarmed by her condition. The woman was hypothermic and nearly unresponsive. The purple streaks had progressed beyond her knee into the fleshy thigh area on her injured leg when Meg checked.

"Whoa, the bite looks disgusting," Bettis said over her shoulder. "And painful. Glad I didn't go wading."

"If you and Mrs. Bettis can sit with her, Red and I need to supervise activities on the beach," Meg said, ignoring his unspoken question.

"Yell for me if there's any change," Red added

"I'm no expert on bite wounds." Doubt radiated from the man.

"I just came along to be out of the sun," Callina rubbed her bare shoulders. "I never had any first aid instructions or anything."

"If she gets agitated, or feverish, or if the appearance of the injury changes," Meg said, forcing herself rein in her impatience. "Call us."

"Right." Bettis dragged a chair next to the couch for himself and another for his wife, as Meg and Red departed.

Not talking, the two of them crossed the landing pad and descended to the beach. To Meg's relief, Mr. Finchon was seated, drinking a large glass of pure whiskey, judging from the translucent bronze color. As Meg approached, he stood, glaring at her, swirling the drink in the heavy crystal goblet. The other passengers gathered nearby, whispering to each other.

"I'm going to start packing up here," Meg said.

"I'm pressing formal negligence charges against you both, as soon as we return to the ship," their Primary guest said, voice quiet and deadly. "And suing the charter company. I'll be transmitting the claims to Sector Hub immediately upon setting foot on the *Far Horizon*."

"Fine, you do whatever you think you need to do," she answered, happy to hear how steady her voice sounded, despite the sinking sensation in her gut. "In the meantime, Mr. Thomsill and I have duties to attend to. Does anyone want another drink or a snack before I close the robos?"

Trever, held up one hand. "Throw me another, but not that swill I endorse. I drink enough of that for the commercials." He guffawed.

Meg fished a high end premixed drink from the robo's storage container and tossed it to the athlete underhanded. He snatched it from the air, reflexes not much diminished from his glory days on an All Sectors professional ball team.

A few other people came forward and she and Red served them. Then the passengers drifted away for the most part. Meg turned her back to the lake and leaned toward Red.

"The Primary's going to be major trouble in about an hour, when the deadline passes with no shuttle arriving," her fellow crew member said before she could utter a word. "Nothing I can't handle easily, as long as the others stay scared sheep."

"I can help with crowd control." She grabbed the bag she'd been guarding, setting it on her prep surface.

He fingered the edge of the cleaning supplies label. "Why do I have hope you're *not* talking about brushes and mops?" he said, moving closer, his body shielding them from casual view.

Opening the bag in such a way as to conceal the contents, she showed him the blasters. "I grabbed these when I went to talk to Drewson."

As he palmed one, Red gave her an awestruck look. "Ma'am, my respect for you has climbed to a whole new level." Efficiently, he checked the charge.

His praise warmed her a bit and settled her nerves. "Taking the weapons was an impulse, but a good precaution, given how strangely the TDJ crew behaved. Don't you want both of them?"

"Do you know how to shoot?"

She nodded. "I've had the basic course."

"Then you keep the other. You're in command here." He slid his blaster into a deep side pocket of his utility pants. "I suggest we keep this advantage our secret until or unless we need to use them, okay?"

"Okay." Following his example, she dropped the second into the pocket of her own pants, sealing the flap.

"Civilian pop guns," he said, "But much, much better than bare fists."

"Is Sharmali going to die?" Meg voiced her biggest fear.

Eyes steady on hers, he nodded once. "I used the only anti-venom inject in the kit already. You saw for yourself how ineffective the dose was. Even if we could get her to the ship in the next half hour, it might already be too late." He touched her elbow lightly. "There's nothing you can do about it. And stop beating yourself up over the sonic barrier in the lake. There was no way for you to know it was off. We all expected it to be on."

Meg disagreed about her own negligence, but now wasn't the time to argue. Squaring her shoulders, she breathed in, counting to ten. Exhaling, she nodded.

"Okay, in an hour, when the deadline passes, plus a margin for error, I'm gathering the group and telling them we believe we're temporarily marooned. Then I want to put them to work. We'll gather all the supplies, including what TDJ left, and we'll move everything to the ranger building. It'll be sunset in a few hours, and I think we'd better spend the night there, don't you?"

"Absolutely." He gestured at the lake. "I assume we can drink this water?"

"Some of the trace chemicals aren't good for humans if we drank it for the rest of our lives, but yes, fine to consume over a short period of time."

"Lock the feelgoods in the bar robo now," he suggested. "I'll go do the same in the TDJ pavilion. Less chance of me having to shoot someone if we don't let the situation degrade to where one or more people are drunk or high." Eyeing the passengers, most of whom were in a tight circle, talking animatedly, he said, "Well, more inebriated than a couple of the men—Trever for one—already are."

"All right." Shading her eyes with one hand, she observed her passengers, her responsibility. She noted with relief that the wandering Sam and Lindy had returned unharmed from their hike, and were the center of the excited circle as the others tried to talk over each other, telling the newcomers the unusual events they'd missed. "I hope at least a few of them are going to pull their own weight."

"People want to eat, they work. Simple as that." Red jogged in the direction of the TDJ site.

CHAPTER TWO

Sharmali died in the middle of the night, quietly, never drawing another breath after one deep inhalation. Meg, who was in the chair next to the couch, drowsing, didn't realize at first her passenger had died. The venom had worked its way through Sharmali's entire body, turning all her veins and arteries a startling black and she'd been breathing shallowly for most of the evening. Meg briefly considered doing CPR, and decided there was no use, given the way the poison had affected the poor woman.

Draping a beach towel over Sharmali's face, Meg sat, head in her hands. There wasn't any point in waking anyone else. Sharmali had no close friends among the passengers. Apparently, she and most of the other women had been hired by the Primary for entertainment thinly veiled as companionship during the cruise. The men were clients and business contacts of Mr. Finchon's, with several of his high level employees along as backup, should any of the discussions delve into business. The Bettises, who'd helped with Sharmali earlier in the day, were the only married couple in the party.

A few passengers had remained aboard the *Far Horizon*, declining the beach party adventure.

Meg glanced to where Mrs. Bettis slept next to her husband. She was Finchon's stepdaughter from his first marriage. Her mother was deceased, but apparently the generational billionaire had promised his late wife to raise her.

As Meg was contemplating what life must have been like for Callina, Red materialized out of the dark, coming inside the lodge from doing a patrol of the grounds. Glancing at the towel over the now deceased passenger's face, he grimaced. He squatted next to Meg's chair. "We'll bury her in the morning," he said, resting his hand on her arm for a moment. "You doing okay?"

She nodded. "You should get some rest," she whispered.

"No worries, I'll cat nap." He rose, stretching from side to side.

She caught his sleeve. "Are you expecting trouble tonight?"

He hesitated. "Honestly? I don't know what to expect. I do know the map in the ranger office shows sonic screens embedded to protect this whole place, which says to me there are land-based predators equivalent to the eel thing I killed earlier. And all of the defenses have been rendered inoperative, apparently during the withdrawal power-down when the rangers left."

"Could be native fauna worse than the eels," she said, trying to remember details from previous visits. The company played down the dangers, for fear of scaring away passengers. The rangers kept the tourist site safe, or used to. "But I don't mean the flora and fauna, I'm talking about why we've been marooned here, why our ship hasn't returned for us."

Red's answer wasn't comforting. "All the things I can think of, based on my previous experience, would be your worst nightmares. Let's just say for now I'm happier patrolling in the dark, and will be ecstatic when the sun rises."

"We were so busy late yesterday, you and I didn't have time to talk privately, or make plans," she said.

"Yeah, we need to figure out our next move, where we go."

"What do you mean? Why can't we stay here? This is where a rescue expedition will expect to find us." Meg wrinkled her brow, trying to comprehend his intentions. "We've got good shelter—we can even open the houses with your special access code. There are edible fish in the lake to supplement my stores, fresh water, all the amenities."

Trever, sprawled atop a stack of beach towels on the floor nearby, rolled over groggily. "Will you two please take it somewhere else so a guy can get some sleep?"

"Sorry, buddy." Red extended his hand to Meg. "Got any real coffee in those robos?"

"Of course." Realizing there was nothing else she could do for Sharmali, she allowed him to draw her to her feet. He led her through the sleeping passengers into the hall and to the kitchen at the rear of the building. Earlier, he'd found a few emergency lamps left in a cupboard, so he flipped one on, setting it on the counter as she activated the robo to brew coffee. "We're marooned now, so there is no crew versus passenger," she said. "All consumables are share and share alike at my discretion."

"All right then, as long as no one is docking my pay." He took the mug with a laugh. "I've missed the real stuff since I left the Teams. Special Forces gets their own allotment. Too pricey to drink much in my new civilian life."

She acknowledged the shared joke from yesterday with a raised eyebrow, and sipped her coffee, but refused to be distracted. "Talk to me. Why are you urging me to move these people somewhere else? And where would we go?"

He leaned against the counter. "We can assume whatever reason the TDJ captain had for leaving was compelling."

She nodded.

"And no sign of Drewson returning." He sipped the hot drink. "The two facts together suggest to me our ship is gone."

"Gone? You mean jumped into hyperspace?"

"Could be." He paused. Meg thought he seemed to be struggling with some inner decision whether to share more of his concerns, so she waited. After a moment, Red said, "The *Far Horizon* could have been destroyed by hostiles."

"An enemy incursion in this Sector?" Meg blinked, trying to assimilate the concept. "Last time I heard any news, the Mawreg were at least two Sectors away, and being pushed back all along the front."

"I don't have any current intel, been out of the Teams too long, but the government never tells civilians the full story about anything." He shook his head. "The fact that the rangers were pulled out of here says a lot to me. And the Mawreg don't usually come in first. The overlords prefer to send one of their client races; the cannon fodder do the heavy lifting of first invasion."

Mind reeling with grim possibilities she'd never considered, Meg pounced on a hole in his logic. "But why attack this planet? It's got no value other than the scenic beauties. No indigenous population. No particularly valuable minerals, despite the pretty colors they add to the water and the tree leaves. Nothing special here to covet."

He drained the last drop of the precious coffee and set the mug on the counter. "I found some kind of research station on one of the maps in the ranger office. Maybe this world has more to it than we know."

This was certainly news to Meg. "Was the research station active? Maybe the staff there can help—"

"Mothballed several years ago according to the note, but it would make a good place for us to wait out our forced shore leave. It's deep in the forest, probably several days walk from here."

"I don't understand why you want us to hike through the undergrowth to reach another abandoned place like this station," Meg said. "Why not stay here in relative comfort?"

"If hostiles are planning to take over this planet, the landing pad and ranger station are visible and vulnerable, too exposed. I'd have preferred to start for the research complex this afternoon, but the idea wasn't workable with the bunch of pampered civilians we've got. When we move out, I'll take or destroy all the maps or references here showing our potential destination. We'll be able to hide there. Once I get you and the others safely established at the site, I'll come back to this area and keep a covert watch for a rescue or the resumption of normal civilian traffic. My best hope is there might be active coms gear at the station so we can call for extraction."

Meg took a shaky breath. "What you're saying makes me want to wake the passengers now and move out in the dark."

Red laid his hand over hers on the counter. "Hey, I'm probably overreacting. Even if hostiles took out the two ships, or were sighted in the vicinity of the system, the enemy might not have any interest in searching for a few stray humans on the surface."

Drawing comfort from his touch, she allowed the contact between them for a moment before withdrawing her hand. Needing to do something with all the nervous energy after this unsettling discussion, she set about packing the robo. "Tell me something, are you normally given to overreacting?" She shot him a glance over her shoulder.

"No."

His answer was what she'd expected. "All right then, let's plan to get organized and hike out of here by noon. I anticipate some serious complaints and foot dragging from the guests, don't you?"

"We'll tell them the truth. And again, the food goes with us, so if the passengers don't relish hunting for their own—"

"Which this crowd is highly unlikely to do." She laughed, guessing he was trying to lighten the atmosphere. As he turned to exit the galley, she said, "Hey, Red?"

"Yeah?" Turning to her, he cocked his head as if he expected some criticism.

"I'm glad you're here with me."

Smiling, he flashed her a sketchy salute.

The guests were a quiet, cowed bunch when Meg woke them at dawn. Serving a bare minimum of food for breakfast, she announced the need for a burial detail to inter poor Sharmali, whose body Red had carried into one of the side offices after their late night chat. The Primary sat in a corner of the conference room, away from the others, Callina fetching food for him. Chewing on a feelgood stick, he scowled, but said nothing.

"Mr. Thomsill and I believe we need to relocate further inland, to another facility we've identified, for our safety," Meg launched into her agenda for their day after all the passengers had plates and were devouring the food she'd measured out. "We'll start hiking there today. After breakfast and the service for Sharmali, I'll need help dividing the supplies into makeshift packs."

The expected uproar took place, with people throwing questions and accusations alike at her.

Oddly enough, Mr. Finchon quelled the discussion before Red had to intervene. The Primary stood and his entourage went quiet as if he'd yelled at them. "I'm taking detailed notes on all of this, for my eventual lawsuit, which I guarantee is going to drive your employer into bankruptcy and ruin the two of you financially for the rest of your lives. You'll never work again, I assure you both." He raised one hand as Red opened his mouth. "Let me finish, Mr. Thomsill. I only want to say this once. I agree with your logic about moving to a less visible location, in case our difficulties of the moment are due to hostile action. Speaking on behalf of my guests and my employees, we'll co-operate with you to the full extent until help arrives." He sat and there was silence for a moment.

"All right then," Meg said, "As soon as breakfast is over, the burial detail goes with Mr. Thomsill and the rest help me pack."

"You guys go ahead and I'll be right out." Red lingered for a moment, stepping close to Meg. Lowering his voice so only she could hear, he said, "Don't lose any sleep over that blowhard's threats. Clearly the situation here falls outside normal cruise conditions and anything he tries to file a lawsuit over will get blown out of court. *Force majeure* and all the old Terran legalese."

Appreciating his concern, she relaxed her tense shoulders and gave him a smile. "Thanks for the reminder. I did know he was blowing smoke, but if thinking about ways to sue us keeps him co-operative, I'm content."

"I should've known you'd be on top of it." Red squeezed her elbow and was gone.

But when she stepped outside with the others later, braced to say a few words over the grave since she was in command, Meg paused on the threshold and scanned the sky.

"Problem?" Red was at her side.

She realized she was getting used to him being there when she needed him. The idea was more comforting than she would have believed possible a few days ago. Pointing with her chin, she said, "See those gray clouds, low on the horizon?"

He followed her line of sight and whistled. "Big storm coming. We were tracking some nasty cells when we landed, but the prevailing winds were blowing out to sea."

"Must have been a shift in the weather then because we're definitely in for it. My landing party was caught here in a freak storm three years ago. It was so bad we couldn't launch. We had to sit it out in the ranger station. Blew for twelve of the longest hours of my life." She didn't add that storms freaked her out, ever since she was a kid.

"On the positive side, we know the ranger station can withstand the winds," he said.

"But we'll never survive in the open. We can't leave today." Meg was surprised to find how much she wanted to get away from the vulnerable facility.

"Well, if the weather's going to be as bad as you're telling me, no one's going to attack us today, either."

The passengers were assembled, so she walked to the flower bed in front of the first small house, which Red had determined was the best spot. Taking a deep breath to calm the fluttering in her gut as she stood by the freshly dug grave, Meg said, "None of us present knew Sharmali Dalgien as anything but a fellow traveler. I've been told she was a good companion, a pleasant person to be with and she didn't deserve to perish here, in such a sad manner. May the Lords of Space speed her on her way and grant her peace."

"Peace," her audience echoed. One or two bowed their heads, praying to their own deities. Lindy, the girl whose face Sharmali had scratched during their spat in the shuttle the day before, wept noisily, although her sobs sounded forced to Meg.

Callina placed hastily plucked wildflowers at the head of the grave.

Harrelly recited a short speech from one of his recent trideo roles, where he'd played a priest in some mythological religion. He took a bow at the end, seeming disappointed no one asked for more. Meg remembered his character had been long-winded in the entertainment feature and supposed they were lucky he gave them one of the briefer, more or less relevant passages.

Much to Meg's surprise, Callina sang, doing a surprisingly professional *a capella* rendition of a popular ballad. The haunting lyrics about a journey and lost love resonated well for the somber occasion. There was applause when she finished the last verse, and then the mourners' attention turned to Meg and Red for direction.

"We can't leave today after all," she said, explaining about the oncoming storm. Just in the time of the brief ceremony, the ominous cloud bank had advanced noticeably closer and a breeze was picking up and eddying the leaves in the yard. "Mr. Thomsill is going to button up the storm shutters pretty soon. For safety reasons, it's essential no one remains outside. We will be setting out promptly at dawn tomorrow, so rest today as much as you can."

Meg tried to prepare them for what the storm would be like, but the ferocity of the winds far exceeded her ability to describe. Lindy became practically catatonic, curled in a chair in the middle of the room, her head covered with a towel, crooning to herself and cringing at the bursts of thunder. The others napped, played desultory card games with the decks Meg had brought on the ill-fated picnic the day before, or else amused themselves with their personal AI's. Callina and her husband sat curled up together on a couch against the far wall, probably happy that while the storm raged, her stepfather couldn't make demands of either one. The sturdily built ranger station rocked under the most ferocious gusts, but despite creaking and groaning, the walls and roof stayed intact.

There was no conversation because it was impossible to be heard over the howling winds.

Meg served lunch when her wrist chrono indicated it was time to eat, and brought dinner later. At least there was no worry over food and drink yet, between her stores and what TDJ had left behind. She fed the crowd a bit extra, hoping the treat would give their spirits a boost.

The Primary played cards with Trever and Harelly for the most part, but occasionally she'd glance up from the book she was merely staring at on her AI, not really reading, and discover Finchon was fixated on her. Eyes glittering, he watched her every move. Finally, she relocated to the kitchen and sat alone. Red checked on her at regular intervals, as he prowled the entire building, on the alert for anything.

He'd been unable to restore full power to the station, telling her the day before several vital parts were missing, apparently removed when the place was abandoned. An independent auxiliary system kept the locks, storm shutters and limited ventilation operational.

Eventually the storm blew itself out, as she'd known it would, but not before there was a crash at the rear of the building that literally shook the ground. Heart pounding, she remembered there'd been an old growth tree shading the station, which evidently had failed to weather one more storm. *Lucky it didn't land on the roof or we'd all be dead.*

As the winds faded in intensity toward evening, she walked into the conference room to check on her passengers. While distributing snacks, she said, "We should be fine now, since the storm is blowing further inland, away from us. Get some sleep and be ready to leave first thing in the morning."

She spent a few moments conversing with Lindy, the woman who'd had such a terrified reaction to the storm, bringing her a cup of tea. After making sure no one else required any special attention, Meg gave Red permission to open the storm shutters on the windows because the ventilation system wasn't working too well and the air had grown stuffy inside the building. He ventured outside and reported there was a great deal of debris on the ground from the winds. The large tree had indeed fallen against the rear of the station, but overall the situation was good.

The night passed without incident. Meg woke at dawn and set out a buffet breakfast, Callina and Red assisting her. As the passengers ate, she said, "I'm going to get a head start on shutting down my robos. We'll be leaving as soon as everyone's done eating breakfast."

"Do you need help?" Red was always attentive.

Callina crammed the remainder of her stale sandwich into her mouth, mumbling something about wanting to pitch in with the chores.

"Don't rush, no need to choke on your food," Meg said with a smile. "We've had enough emergencies for one trip. This is routine, done it a million times, but thanks for the offer of help, both of you. It'll take me five minutes or less, promise."

CHAPTER THREE

The enemy attacked just as Meg disappeared into the hallway to the kitchen. Red hit the deck, dragging Callina with him as the windows burst inwards, showering reinforced glass on the occupants of the room. As if in slow motion, projectiles hit the floor, each bursting into flame upon landing. Vivid yellow and red fire spread from the impact points, creating a firestorm in the room. A projectile landed right next to Lindy, who was immediately enveloped in flame, the blanket she'd been wrapped in going up in an instant. She was dead before she could extricate herself from the folds. Sam and several of the others were trapped on the far side of the room, flames surrounding them on all sides. Yelling and shouting, they attempted to beat the fire out with cushions. Finding new fuel in the furniture, the blaze engulfed them in an explosion.

Heart pounding, Red spared a second to glance at the last spot he'd seen Meg. Through the smoke and flames, he caught a glimpse of her standing in the hallway, screaming his name. He had no way to get there, although he took a step toward her. The center of the room was an inferno. Part of the roof collapsed, sending a solid sheet of sparks flying through the room, forcing him to retreat.

Callina was hanging onto his shirt, coughing. "We have to get out."

With one final despairing glance at the raging blaze where Meg had been standing, he drew his blaster, scooped the younger woman into his arms, and sprinted for the front door. Most likely, he was going to run right into the waiting enemy, but the only other choice was burning to death. Carrying Callina, he hurdled the low flames at the threshold and rolled onto the porch to extinguish any stray sparks on their clothing. The blaster was knocked from his hand by the impact, flying into the darkness.

Releasing Callina, he yelled at her. "Run to the trees."

Eyes wide, she nodded, gathering herself to obey. Before she could move, a sticky white net enveloped them, head to toe. A moment later, both net and prisoners were dragged ruthlessly off the porch, bumping across the ground.

He was well aware that the more he struggled, the tighter the net would become, so he forced himself to stay still, and told the screaming woman to do the same. This was a favorite weapon of the Shemdylann pirates. He'd been imprisoned in one before, during training, and knew there was no escape short of burning free with a blaster. His arms were pinned to his sides at awkward angles and struggling would only constrict the cords until he became unconscious or died.

So intent was he on not triggering the web to strangle them, he was startled when a voice spoke right above them. "An amusing diversion, like stepping on a nalirva hive and watching the bugs scurry in a futile attempt to survive. Truly unexpected entertainment."

The words were in passable Basic. The Shemdylann pirate standing next to them was a high ranking officer, judging by the insignia tattooed onto his upper mandible.

"There are more people inside, you bastard," Red said. His head pounded with the anger and grief surging through his body. Lying there as a helpless prisoner while innocent people died a few feet away tore at him.

The Shemdylann waved one clawed hand. "Then let them come outside, or die. I care not. Either way will be equally pleasing to my crew and me."

The screams from whoever was trapped in the burning building continued for a few more moments, before the entire structure collapsed in an explosion of flame and sparks, bringing abrupt silence rather than the crackling of the fire. Heartsick and consumed with grief for Meg, Red tried to reassure and comfort Callina as much as he could in the impossible situation. She managed to hook three fingers around his left hand and he squeezed tight. "Don't look at the cabin, best to close your eyes."

Apparently deciding there was no more amusement to be gleaned, the pirate officer moved away from the net confining Red and Callina. "Bring the prisoners to the beach," he said, still in Basic. "We'll see what exactly we've captured and decide what to do with them."

A moment later, a pirate soldier scooped up the double burden as if the net and its contents weighed nothing, hoisting them a good eight feet off the ground onto its shoulder. Carrying them with ease, the alien took the path toward the lake. Head down over his captor's spiny mantle, Red couldn't do much more than endure the next few moments until they were tossed carelessly onto the sand by the lake. Fortunately, the way he was trapped in the coils of the net, he cushioned Callina's fall. He heard thuds and cries of pain or protest as a few other prisoners were deposited close by. Craning his neck painfully, he found the Primary in the net next to him on one side.

Figures that guy would survive, while Meg…he forced himself to redirect his thoughts. "Hey, how you holding up?" he asked Callina.

"I-I'm okay. What are they going to do with us?" she whispered.

"Hard to say. I'll protect you as much as I can." He made the promise, knowing full well there might not be anything he could do. "Our treatment will depend on what brought the Shemdylann here."

"Silence." The closest guard kicked sand at them, and Red closed his eyes against the shower of grit.

A few moments later the sticky webbing dissolved, as a Shemdylann soldier passed a light emitter over them, set to the proper frequency to counteract the coils. Before he could make a move to do anything, Red was pinioned from behind by one alien, while another dragged Callina by her hair into a position next to him. He and the other survivors were in a line, seven altogether, facing the insect-like Shemdylann officer, lounging in a complicated seat brought for him by his subordinates. A lower-ranking officer stood behind the chair, waiting to carry out any orders. Shemdylann by the dozens bustled to and fro on the beach, setting up some kind of apparatus, more of the strange chairs, and performing other tasks. One or two of the hulking, dark red-and-black creatures had wandered into the lake to their double-jointed knees and were staring at the Falls. Assessing the odds, Red took note of the three large craft crowding the landing pad. Too many to all be from one ship, unless it was a battlecruiser. The Shemdylann must have a major presence in this planetary system.

"I didn't expect to gather slaves here, did you?" The commander spoke over his shoulder to the waiting officer.

"A bonus," the subordinate said, snapping his mandibles in apparent pleasure.

The Shemdylann in charge waved one appendage at the prisoners. "Remove your outer clothing, humans, in order for me to assess your value."

Glancing at each other as if for courage, most of the group prepared to obey the order. Mr. Finchon stepped forward.

"What are you doing? Don't provoke them." His stepdaughter grabbed his elbow.

Shaking off her grip, he adopted his usual arrogant stance and said, "I invoke the rules of the Freemarket Repatriation Pact." Chest puffed, chin jutting, he waved his right wrist. "I have the terms here, on an embedded chip."

"What's he talking about?" Red asked Mr. Bettis, who was standing on the other side of Callina.

"Like an insurance policy, very hush-hush. Some of the wealthiest in the Sectors paid through a broker on Freemarket for the right to be ransomed rather than killed or enslaved in the event of capture by the Shemdylann," Finchon's assistant replied.

"Now, this is intriguing," the commander was saying, clicking his mandibles. "Bring him to me. If you lie, human, your death will be protracted and entertaining for my crew."

"No lie." Not waiting for escort, Finchon strutted to a position in front of the chair and stood motionless as his wrist was scanned by a subordinate who rushed forward, instrument in one pincer. "I'm Ahmeril Finchon and I like to know who I'm dealing with. You are?"

Making the guttural cawing sound that was a Shemdylann laugh, the officer said, "Like all of your kind, you believe in your own importance, despite the evidence to the contrary." Tapping his clawed toes on the sand, he studied the scanner as his soldier held it close. "Hmm, I'll make a tidy profit on this trip besides the other rewards. Congratulations, human, you do have the prepaid right to transmit a hefty ransom through the Freemarket broker." Opening a pouch at his belt, the commander withdrew a chain made from intricate silver links, with one cuff at the end. Leaning forward, he snapped the shackle over Finchon's left wrist, saying as he attached the other end to a loop piercing his carapace, "You'll stay with me at all times, both for your protection and to ensure I collect my reward. And I, by the way, am Captain Ar-Taan-Crxtahl, since you have such a desire to know who holds your fate in his claws." The alien yanked on the chain slightly and cackled anew.

Biting his lip, the billionaire regarded the cuff with distaste, turning it on his wrist with one finger, but said nothing.

"Sir," the soldier with the scanner said, "According to the terms of the agreement, he also paid for the right to ransom anyone else he chooses."

"A well thought out codicil," said the commander. "I applaud you. Are there any among this clump of humans you wish to add to the deal? At full price, of course."

Finchon turned on his heel in the sand and frowned at his fellow prisoners, assessing each one in turn. Red spat, full of contempt, as his eyes met the billionaire's. Rubbing his chin where he'd been punched the day before, Finchon tightened his thin lips and moved on to Callina. He regarded her for a moment, then turned to his captor. "No one else."

Mrs. Bettis screamed and the other three surviving male passengers cursed. Harrelly fell to his knees in the sand, begging for mercy.

Red said, "You son of a bitch, how can you abandon your daughter to these monsters? At least pay her ransom."

"She's not my daughter, only a kid my late first wife brought along into our marriage. I paid her way for the past fifteen years." He made a thumbs down sign. "Now I'm done. The price is too high. You have no idea how many credits the ransom is. Let her husband take care of her."

Red put an arm around Callina. Clinging to his side, sniffling, she said to her stepfather, "I never trusted you. I hate you!"

"I'm sure you do. You've outlived your usefulness to me, and we both know it." Unfazed, Finchon turned to the Shemdylann. "We're done. I'll transmit the ransom payment order to New Switzerland as soon as you like."

"A respectable decision in all aspects. We eat our young at times," the officer said, eyeing Callina.

A Shemdylann soldier came rushing up, saluting. "Sir, we found a weapon in the brush beside the burnt building." He passed the small civilian blaster to his superior.

"Ah, so one of you is a warrior of sorts. Who does this toy belong to?"

Red didn't see any point in denial. He raised his hand. "It was mine, from our shuttle."

"Wise choice, to answer me promptly. No punishment for this then—I can be merciful." Crxtahl waved the soldier away and leaned forward in his chair, addressing the prisoners. "We're wasting daylight. Remove your clothing as instructed."

The male passengers peeled off their shirts and pants, and stood in their swimming gear. Red had worn swim trunks under his uniform the day before in case any of the guests wanted to go snorkeling.

Callina pulled off her sundress, revealing a frilly yellow one-piece bathing suit.

As if bored, the Shemdylann leader accepted a container from an aide and took a long pull of whatever the fluid refreshment was. As he tossed the now-empty package at the waiting soldier, he said, "Bring the warrior to me."

A guard pinched his claws none too gently into Red's upper arm and half dragged him to the officer's chair, where Crxtahl studied the intricate black tattoos looping around his shoulder and down his spine, making Red turn so he could trace the design with one claw. Red stood at attention as the alien stared at him after the thorough examination. "Explain the markings."

Easing into parade rest, Red pitched his voice in a casual tone. "I'm a sailor, sailors get tattoos. I liked the design and I was drunk that night. End of story." He wasn't going to explain the dragon was the symbol of Team Twelve. If the Shemdylann found out who he was, things would go from bad to worse, and he was determined to stay alive long enough to get revenge for Meg's death, not to mention trying to protect Callina. He'd do what he could for the others, but the one surviving woman had to be the priority. Good thing he'd kept his mouth shut on the cruise about his military background. People could make guesses, but no one had certain knowledge. Other than Meg, and she was dead. Thinking of Meg pierced his heart with fresh grief. He nearly missed the Shemdylann's next comment.

"Well, you'll make a fine slave, well-muscled for a human. The markings add interest. You'll bring a high price in the markets." A casual wave of the captain's mandible brought two soldiers to hustle Red back into line, where Callina took his hand. She looped her arm through her husband's, as if she needed support from both of them to remain on her feet. Red guessed her stepfather's refusal to ransom either of them had been a severe blow, no matter how much bad blood there might have been between them up to this moment.

One at a time the others were brought forward, but the examination of them was more cursory and the commander didn't appear impressed, although Trever rated a closer look, in carefully maintained athletic shape from his playing days. The pirate didn't bother inspecting Callina at all. "Not the best lot, but then, we didn't come here expecting to bag any slaves at all. Cage them."

Guards shoved them all into a shimmering energy cage set off to the western end of the beach. Their clothes were tossed in before the entrance to the cell was closed. Red grabbed his uniform and shrugged into it as fast as he could, confirming as he did so that all the useful items in his pockets had been confiscated. Callina retrieved her sundress and she and her husband moved to the rear of the cage, sitting next to Red.

"I'm sorry about Meg," she said, patting his hand. "I liked her."

"Yeah, me too." It was going to be a long time, if ever, before the ache in his heart over losing Meg went away. "I'm sorry your stepdad is being such a prick about the ransom. Maybe he'll change his mind."

She looked down the beach to where Finchon sat at ease, demeanor as cool as if he was still in charge, despite being tethered by seven feet of chain to the alien commander. "No," she said, shaking her head, "He won't. When my Mom died, his PR people told him at the funeral I was good for his image, made the public think he was nice. I heard them talking. 'Humanized' him was what the head PR lady said. His image is why he always took me on his trips, instead of sending me away to school like he promised Mom when she got sick. He'll get sympathy for losing his precious daughter and son-in-law to the aliens on their honeymoon."

Sarcasm was apparent in her tone. "No one will ever be able to say any different. We're not going to survive, are we?"

He assessed the energy field surrounding them, humming and slightly distorting the view. "Too soon to tell." While on the planet, there was a hope, however faint, he might be able to catch a break, grab her, and make it to the jungle. With his specialized skills, he could hide and protect Callina as well. If he stayed free long enough, the Shemdylann might abandon the chase for both of them, and go on about their business.

"I don't want to be a slave," she said softly, drawing circles in the sand with one fingertip. She brushed away a tear with the back of her other hand. "And I don't want to be eaten."

He nudged her shoulder with his own. "Hey, Crxtahl was talking about Shemdylann hatchlings, not humans."

"Oh." She seemed a bit comforted by the correction.

He didn't tell her there were definite rumors in the fleet attesting to Shemdylann considering humans a delicacy. They'd both be dead long before anything like that could happen. Red could break her neck with one quick move, and he himself had the checkout code, as the Teams referred to it—a psychic implant he could activate to suicide.

Had permanent orders to use it, in fact, if "irretrievably in the grip of enemy forces."

Standing Order One.

Harsh to the nonmilitary mind, no doubt, Red was comfortable with it. A man didn't go downrange without making peace with his own mortality. You couldn't do the things Special Forces often did if you were worried about your own life or death. And as an operator, he knew too many pieces of useful classified information to let the enemy take him alive.

The situation wasn't irretrievable yet, however, not by a long shot.

"What are the pirates doing?" Callina asked, breaking into his thoughts.

Stretching, Red stood to see how their captors were passing their leisure time. The beach was literally crawling with Shemdylann now. Some were engaged in mock battles, cheered on by throngs of their comrades. Others were splashing in the lake. A fire pit had been dug and a crew of five aliens was doing some serious cooking, as if catering a banquet. Many of the aliens were basking in the sun, extended neck frills pulsing in the heat. And a few were entwined in clusters of four to six, tentacles and other sinuous organs busily at work.

"I think the pirates are on shore leave," he said, hardly believing it. There'd never been any record of such activity, but what other conclusion could he draw? "Hey, pal," he yelled at the guard standing by their cage. "What brings you guys here?"

The guard was watching the cluster of copulating Shemdylann, his neck frill extended and pulsing red. Apparently, no one had told him not to talk to the prisoners because he said, "We've been in heavy combat, penetrating this Sector. Our officers said this planet was a fabled human resort and he would bring us here for a day or two of reward, if we defeated the enemy ships. We'll regain energy for the next assault, on your Sector Hub, to be launched when we receive further orders from the Mawreg."

Red affected astonishment. "You brought everybody here to party, leaving your ship uncrewed?"

"Fool, of course not." The coarse spines covering the alien's carapace bristled and he stood taller. "You ask too many questions." He sidestepped, pivoting in the sand to watch his fellow pirates cavorting. In Shemdylann, he grumbled to himself. "Five ships and a battle cruiser full of troops, lots drawn across the fleet for who would be lucky enough to enjoy the day on the planet. I pay a hefty bribe to win a spot and now I must stand here, watching over vermin, while my fellow soldiers *shi tangor dunac midtahnn.*"

Red gave no outward sign of comprehension, although he spoke fluent Shemdylann. Leaving the increasingly agitated guard alone, he retreated to the rear of the cage and pondered the intel he'd gathered. Not that there was any way for him to pass the information to the Sectors' military authorities.

"Please, isn't there something you can do to help us?" Eyes wide, Callina pleaded with him. "Isn't there some way we can escape? Can't you get us out of here?"

He tried to be polite. "Lady, these are the Shemdylann, in case you haven't noticed. They only respond to overwhelming force, or heaps of credits. Your stepfather Finchon is the only one here with enough gravity to pay their demands. I'm just a working stiff, out of luck, like you."

"Friend, yeah, the son of a bitch claimed to be my friend all right," said Harelly, standing next to her. "He always wanted me to come along on these trips of his, impress the clients with his famous actor friends. Not so much now." He laughed bitterly. "What's going to happen to us?"

Basics from past briefings surfaced in Red's mind. "Cryo sleep once we reach their ship." He personally had no intention of surviving to leave the planet. Lords of Space bless the checkout code.

"And then?" asked Mr. Bettis, holding his sobbing wife.

"You heard the commander." Red had no interest in trying to cheer his fellow prisoners with lies or half-truths. "The Shemdylann are going to sell us for slaves, in the Outlier Empire most likely, or on one of their own worlds. The life of a slave tends to be short and brutal. She might do better, since she can sing. Be sure to tell them about your voice, lady."

"You're remarkably calm about it." Trever studied Red's face. "What do you know that you aren't telling us?"

Harelly moved closer, like a dog on a scent. "Yeah, you were ship's crew, you must have some inside info."

Belatedly, Red remembered these men were accustomed to reading people and situations. He didn't trust them not to sell him out in a heartbeat, if either realized doing so would give them an advantage with the Shemdylann. Finchon had already proven how little other human beings meant to men of his ilk. These two had the misfortune of not being in his extreme wealth bracket.

"Saving my strength in case I get a break. Panic doesn't do any good. A cool head might." He settled into a more comfortable position, acting casual. "Hey, you're both wealthy, right? You can try negotiating for ransom yourself."

"I don't come close to Finchon's generational billions of credits," Harelly answered, lips thinned as if he'd swallowed something bitter. "My trideos make piles of credits, but I have expenses to match. I was never invited to join the Freemarket Pact."

"Very few were," said Trever, staring at Finchon lounging down the beach.

The conversation having run its course, the remaining humans sat or laid in their enclosure. Red assessed the Shemdylann and made plans. As the food was served to the alien troops, strangely shaped containers of glowing red liquid were also handed out. Based on the way the Shemdylann were reacting as they guzzled the stuff, he guessed it was a feelgood. He didn't know whether to hope Crxtahl could maintain control of the increasingly rowdy warriors or not.

At least one mock combat ended in death or injury as the afternoon wore on, and the crowd yelled for more as the corpse was dragged to the side of the beach.

He played tic tac toe in the sand with Callina until she dozed off from exhaustion and the effects of the sun beating directly on them. Their captors gave them no water or food.

Somewhere in midafternoon, Red noticed a clump of the inebriated aliens gathered beside the rotting remains of the eel he'd killed. Was it just two days ago? The Shemdylann behaved in a highly agitated manner, gesturing for more of their comrades to join them. When the commander strolled to the edge of the water, there was a long conversation, punctuated by much gesticulation, including soldiers pointing at the cage. Adrenaline spiking to meet the challenge he was sure was coming, he got to his feet, urging a drowsy, confused Callina to stand behind him.

Startled, the others gazed in every direction, trying to figure out what had set Red into motion.

Suddenly, four Shemdylann came striding through the sand directly to the cage, talking excitedly in their own language. Red caught fragments, something about a rare delicacy in the lake and the need for bait.

The guard barred their way. "Stand down," said the officer in the lead, speaking Shemdylann. "We've permission to take one human as bait, for sport. Now, open the cage."

"Him," said a soldier, neck frill opening and closing as he rocked unsteadily on his clawed feet. "The warrior." He was pointing at Red. "He'll last the longest."

"Fool, weren't you listening? Ar-Taan-Crxtahl said anyone but him. He'll fetch a good price."

Red tensed, pulling Callina to stand in front of him. He rested his hands casually on her shoulders for a moment before curling his fingers around her neck as she watched him.

"Mr. Thomsill?"

"Our captors are going to play some unpleasant, ultimately fatal games, and I won't let it be with either you or me," he whispered, barely moving his lips. A flicker of what he hoped was comprehension shone in her blue eyes for a moment before she looked at the sand. "If the soldiers pick either of us, we won't be alive to see what happens next."

"Okay," she said, swallowing hard. "You—you'll make it quick, won't you?"

"No pain, I promise." He waited. If the enemy intended to take her—or him—both would be dead in the next minute. Mercy killing and suicide were preferable to what the Shemdylann had in mind for whoever was chosen to "amuse" the crowd.

She closed her eyes.

"The older one then," said the eager warrior, pointing at Harelly, closest to the door. "He'll bring the least as a slave, no muscles or meat."

"Agreed."

Before Red could say or do anything, the energy door had dimmed for a moment and the hapless actor was plucked from the enclosure by the Shemdylann's tentacles. The energy pulsed to renewed life at the entrance and all the aliens headed for the beach, dragging the human with them, poking and prodding him with the tips of their pincers.

"Don't look," Red told Callina as he searched their cage fruitlessly for something to attempt disrupting the energy loop with. This was their chance, with the guard gone and the crowd distracted.

He glanced over his shoulder as two Shemdylann inflicted long, shallow cuts on the screaming human's arms and legs with the rough edges of their pincers before flinging him into the lake. As Harelly attempted to rise, someone else pushed him further into the water with a splash. Out in the center of the lake, Red observed several rippling vees, as the big eels caught the scent of blood.

At least the venom would render the poor passenger unconscious pretty efficiently once the attack started.

He heard Bettis retch.

Filled with adrenaline and determined not to lose this chance to escape, Red fell to his knees and began digging under the energy wall, hoping perhaps it didn't go all the way to bedrock. Callina joined him, as did the others. Sand flew. The small trench deepened to four inches, then six, but the energy's shimmer resisted any attempt to push so much as a finger to freedom. Red stopped excavating for a moment, grabbing Callina and yanking her to her feet.

"You keep an eye on what the soldiers are doing, there at the waterfront. Tell me the instant any of the bastards turn in our direction."

She gulped. "I can't watch—"

He shook her so hard her teeth rattled. "That poor guy is dying right now to give us a chance here. We can't waste it. Now open your damn eyes and report to me when the enemy moves. Look at them, not him."

Swallowing hard, wiping blood off her lip from where she'd bitten herself, she said, "Okay, okay."

"I think we might be getting to the edge," her husband called. "The light's weaker."

"Keep your voice low, some of them speak Basic." He sprinted to help with the frantic digging.

CHAPTER FOUR

The concussion of the windows breaking and the fire bombs hitting the floor left Meg frozen in shock for a moment, hands over her ears against the awful sound. Flame squirted across the floor right in front of her, blazing waist high. Screaming Red's name, she retreated in the only direction she could go, down the hall to the kitchen. Fire was licking at the doorway to the conference room as she ducked inside the kitchen to grab the nearest pack, sweep the map to the research station into the bag, and take the large knife she'd been using to slice meat for sandwiches. Preparing to flee out the rear door of the station, she turned and froze.

Too late. Pausing those few seconds to grab the items she needed had given the alien fire time to fill the hall. How the seven hells could the stuff move so fast? The heat and smoke were overpowering. Already burning, the entrance to the kitchen and the hall beyond were impassable, a solid pit of flames. She heard the structure creaking under the assault. An ugly tongue of red and yellow ran from the top of the door across the ceiling toward her, fat sparks dropping to ignite new blazes.

Pulse pounding, grabbing a towel from the stash in the robo to put over her mouth and nose to block the smoke, she retreated. She dropped to the floor to get below the smoke as best she could, and crawled to the end of the small kitchen. Scrabbling desperately at the wall, she felt her fingers slide over a crack, and she remembered there was a door to some kind of storage space. Crouching, she managed to get the portal open and slipped through, slamming it shut against the fire.

The storage space was blessedly smoke free for the moment, although ghostly gray tendrils seeped through the narrow crack in the portal. Meg retreated, sucking in cleaner air, searching frantically for her next move. The outer wall had a window, a webbed crack running from edge to edge, probably from the impact of the tree falling during the night. She grabbed a chair from the small desk wedged into the corner of the room, and pounded on the glass.

Three times she slammed the chair into the reinforced portal. On the fourth attempt, her arms losing strength as the room filled with smoke, the glass gave way, shattering outward in all directions. Climbing onto the chair, Meg dropped her pack outside and then attempted to crawl out the window. Branches from the fallen tree blocked her path. Desperate, she shimmied through a space between the branches and fell hard. Dazed for a moment, coughing, she realized she was lying in a nest of wet foliage, between several more branches. She was sure she had cuts, but there was no time to do anything but keep moving. Grabbing the straps of the backpack, she slung it on her shoulders. Trying to control her trembling limbs, she crawled through a seemingly endless maze of broken wood and slimy leaves, heading away from the building.

At least the dampness of the fallen tree might keep it from catching fire.

Behind her, she heard an explosion as the ranger station fell in on itself, she assumed. Ahead, she could see the edge of the branches and she froze. Where she was, in the midst of tree debris, she hoped she was impossible to see with the naked eye. Would whoever had attacked them think to search with more sensitive technology? Would the enemy even know she was alive?

She backtracked a few feet, nestling under a particularly dense area of the branches, and curled up, trying not to cry. For a few moments, Meg had to work hard to quell the terror. Controlling her breathing and forcing herself to recall the recipe for the most complicated mixed feelgood drink she'd learned at school helped. Anything to get her whirling thoughts under control. She kept seeing Red's face as he'd called out to her across the barrier of flames. Had he escaped?

Better not to think about him right now.

Blood was mixed with the rain on her hand, providing a trail the enemy could easily follow. Carefully, she worked the backpack off and opened the flap, digging for the small medkit. As best she could, she bandaged the worst scrapes and cuts, and then made herself swallow a small container of energy drink. Her stomach rebelled, but Meg breathed deep and concentrated until the nausea had passed. The thick liquid coated her throat, soothing her cough as well.

She decided the first priority was to get away from the ranger station and take refuge in the forest itself. Then she could figure out her next steps. Cautiously, moving a few inches at a time, keeping the huge trunk between herself and the ranger station, she worked her way to the edge of the fallen tree's canopy. She'd have to cross ten feet of clear space stretching between her and the beginning of the forest. Turning her head in all directions, she blinked and froze at the terrifying reality of three alien craft sitting on the landing pad. She'd no idea what species of sentients owned the ships, but she'd never seen anything like them at any Sector's port.

Something cold rasped across her leg and Med stifled a scream as one of the large tree serpents undulated its endless coils over her, on its way somewhere else and apparently not hungry, thankfully. She'd have to be more careful. The aliens weren't the only menace out here. But watching the snake slither toward the trees and then coil itself around the nearest trunk, ascending impossibly fast in a blur of color, gave her an idea.

"You're going to run to the next tree and you're going to climb like hell, and you're going to make it, Meg Antille," she said to herself. "If Red, or anyone else is still alive, you're their only hope right now."

She crouched under the leafy branches, trying to be as sure as possible no one was close by. Taking deep breaths, she remembered her father's advice to her brothers and her, on more than one hunting expedition, that rapid movement attracts attention. He wouldn't approve of her current plan. But there was absolutely no cover between her and the forest, and she didn't think she had the nerve to creep to safety inches at a time right now. With a whispered, "Sorry, Dad," she counted to three under her breath, and burst out of hiding, sprinting into the shelter of the forest. As soon as she passed the tree line, all the time expecting to be shot in the back, she leaped to grab a low hanging limb and climbed from branch to branch as fast as she could. She didn't allow herself to stop until she was high above the ground, deep into the overlapping branches of the forest. Then she sank against the tree trunk, leaning on its reassuring bulk, and considered her next move.

With a start, she realized she'd nodded off or passed out. Vertigo assailed her as she glanced down. Trying to orient herself, she realized the network of huge branches, four to eight feet wide in places, would provide her a highway in the sky, if she moved carefully. It might not occur to aliens to search the foliage above them for a human, but she needed to be quiet and stay as hidden as she could. No overconfident moves.

"I have to know what's happening to Red and the others," she said under her breath.

She took a deliberate moment to organize her few possessions. Tucking the knife in her belt, she drew the blaster, checking the charge. About eighty percent, but better than nothing. Her sturdy work shoes gave her good purchase on the damp branches.

By the time she navigated to a spot where she could see the imploded, smoldering ranger station far below, no one was left there, not human or alien. Flashes of color and voices in an unknown language off to the east attracted her attention. Puzzled as to why the invaders would be going to the beach, she searched her memory, reassured by the mental picture of how the forest grew nearly to the edge of the sand.

I can get pretty close, see what's going on. Check for the others. She heard her father's voice in her head, lecturing her brothers and herself to always evaluate all the options in a situation, not jump at the first one that came to mind.

Was there another option in this case? For a moment, she considered the research installation, three days' hike away in the forest. If she left now, she could probably get there with no problem. Apparently, no one was searching for her. Even her companions must have assumed she was dead in the wreckage of the ranger station. But leaving aside her refusal to abandon Red if he was alive, not to mention any remaining passengers, what would she do at the other facility? She couldn't even open the doors—*she* didn't have any mysterious, all access code.

Hence, no way to call for help from off planet. The only sensible choice was to continue what she was doing and try not to get caught.

Having decided, and not planning to revisit the other options, she walked along the tree branches, gaining confidence as she went, but slipping often enough to banish cockiness. When she came as close as she dared to go to the beach, she was astonished to find the entire space occupied by large aliens, apparently relishing a day of relaxation. Several hundred of them roamed along the lakeshore.

Her attention was caught by the sight of her fellow humans, standing in a line in front of what must be the alien leader. So few! She caught her breath as a nearly naked Red, identifiable from this distance by his hair, was dragged forward and examined at length by his captor. She wished for distance viewers, but the pack didn't contain any. Heart pounding, clutching the blaster in one hand, she chewed her knuckle to keep from screaming as the aliens manhandled him. Frantic with worry, Meg relaxed a bit as Red was allowed to retreat, standing beside a shorter person who must be Callina.

At least the six survivors appeared unharmed so far.

Identifying Finchon by his red and white jacket, she took note of how he was singled out for some kind of special treatment, separated from the others. "Could be good, could be bad," she whispered to herself.

She watched as Red and the remaining passengers were marched down the beach toward her. She shrank lower amongst the foliage, but none of the aliens glanced up. The humans were shoved into some kind of glowing cage and left with only one guard.

Frustration ate at Meg as the day wore on. So close and yet so far! She couldn't develop any plan offering a chance of success. She'd no idea where the vulnerable points were on an alien's naturally armored body. Pacing on the tree limb, she debated whether a blaster shot could even pierce the carapace? And if she did kill or disable the single guard, there were hundreds more aliens nearby. Squinting, she noted the Primary getting special treatment, even from the enemy, and his status made her angry. She'd pretty much decided to creep up on the cage from the rear if the humans remained on the beach after dark fell, and use the blaster to disrupt the energy field. At least a few people—Red for sure—might make it to the shelter of the forest and escape.

She stayed hydrated and forced herself to consume a sandwich, even though the food threatened to choke her in her current stressed condition. Guilt dampened her appetite, knowing the captives weren't being given anything, not even water, but she had to stay strong for the rescue attempt. Her cuts and bruises ached and she had a first degree burn on her lower right leg. A headache started over her left eye and there was nothing in the meager first aid kit to help. Small insects seemed unable to resist her where she sat among flowering vines, but she needed the cover in case any of the enemy glanced her way.

The sun would be setting soon. She stood slowly on the broad branch and made sure her backpack was secure, the knife and blaster safely fastened to her belt. Then she descended the far side of the tree, away from the beach, getting ready for her rescue attempt.

As she crept around the base of the trunk a few moments later, the situation on the beach had changed for the worse. A cluster of aliens stood at the door to the cage and as she watched, soldiers dragged Harelly away. Transfixed for a moment, watching Red and the others digging frantically, she forced herself into motion, running forward, blaster aimed at the nearest corner of the energy cage. She'd no idea what the weapon's effective distance was.

Kneeling at the edge of the sand, hoping the spot was close enough, she took aim and a blaster bolt sizzled, striking a glancing blow. The cage popped and disappeared in a shower of sparks. Immediately, Red was sprinting toward her, carrying Callina, the other two humans doing their best to keep up. He held out one hand. "Weapon?"

She tossed him the blaster, turning to flee herself.

"Lady, you're a sight for sore eyes," he said, not breaking stride.

"We can climb—" she said in between breaths.

"No time, better to get as far into the forest as we can, then go aloft."

He led the way, plunging into the underbrush. Meg ran right behind him, as fast as she could, along a creek bed. After a few moments of this, Red veered inland away from the waterway.

Behind her, she heard angry yelling in an alien language and a barrage of blaster shots. The aliens were shooting into the forest somewhat eastward of their true location.

As if the fusillade had been a signal, Red stopped at the base of a giant old growth tree, forty feet in circumference. "Now we climb. Lead the way, Meg."

She didn't hesitate, leaping to catch the first branch, getting her balance atop the limb, Meg looked down. "Come on, come on." Impatience and fear made her jittery and brusque. Trever made the ascent with surprising speed and kept going without saying a word to Meg as he brushed past her.

There was no one immediately after him. Hand clenched on a sturdy bark protuberance, fighting a touch of vertigo, Meg forced herself to check on the people below. "What's the delay now?"

Callina was on her knees on the ground, one hand pressed to her side. "I can't climb a tree, are you people crazy?"

"Climb or die; it's simple." Tilting his head, Red told Meg, "Don't wait, keep going higher. I'll need room on the branch for these two."

"Right." She followed the route Trever had taken, hard as it was to make herself leave Red.

Taking a break at the next branch to check on the passengers' progress, she was encouraged to find Bettis had his wife's arm, trying to get her to her feet. "You can do it, honey. The stewardess is doing it."

Red made it easily to the first branch. Kneeling, one hand locked on the bark, he stretched the other hand toward Mrs. Bettis. "Last chance, lady. Take my hand now and I'll get you started. We're not going to carry you and I'm not waiting for you. You can try running through the forest if you want."

She stared to the north, as if staying on the ground appealed to her. She took a half step.

Her husband restrained her. "But we'll die, right?" Bettis said, craning his neck to stare at Red.

"Or get recaptured, and I don't think the Shemdylann are going to be in a good mood." Red turned to follow Meg and Trever.

The idea of him abandoning them seemed to galvanize the reluctant Mrs. Bettis. "Wait, wait, I'll do it, I'll do it." She stretched one hand toward Red beseechingly, rising on her tiptoes.

"Keep your voice down." Red grabbed her arms as her husband boosted her, and a moment later she was on the branch. Bettis scrambled awkwardly, his flimsy beach shoes slipping on the bark as he sought footholds. "You might do better barefoot than with those." Shaking his head, Red pointed his finger at the man for emphasis. "Your wife's your responsibility. I can't set a slower pace for the two of you."

"I understand. We'll do our best." Bettis puffed his chest out. "I jog every morning in the executive exercise suite back at corporate HQ."

Not answering, apparently having said all he was going to on the subject, Red ascended the tree. Meg had already walked carefully along a huge branch to the next tree and was waiting for him. Trever stood off to the side, tapping his foot impatiently. Red ran across the branch like it was nothing and caught Meg by the waist, giving her a smacking kiss on the lips before releasing her. "I thought you were dead."

"I was afraid you were," she replied, a little dazed. "Then I worried about you all day, stuck in that cage."

"It was like being in an old fashioned zoo, or a jail from the history trideos." Callina gave a nervous-sounding giggle from where she clung to the tree, taking a break from climbing. "But scary."

Red sighed. "No time to talk right now. Keep moving, don't wait for the Bettises if they can't keep up, and don't wait for me. I'll double back on occasion to see what the enemy is doing but I'll rejoin you, no problem."

"Promise?" The idea of losing him again made Meg nauseous.

"Don't worry; I'm a hard man to lose. Go generally west." He shook a finger at Callina. "And be quiet."

"Right." Meg pointed to the next branch and the woman started walking. Red touched her elbow. "And, Meg? This was an inspired idea. Shemdylann aren't too smart and may never think to check in the trees."

Warmed by his praise, she followed Trever along the maze of interlocking branches, high above the forest floor. Sneezing occasionally, the athlete stayed ahead of her, complaining when he had to backtrack if Meg decided another path was safer to follow.

Meg's thighs ached as if she'd hiked along the branches for hours before Red called a halt. She tried to stay fit while on the cruises she worked, but clearly she hadn't been exercising hard enough. Of course, she'd never expected to be called upon to traverse the planet on foot.

All five of them huddled against a massive tree trunk, hundreds of feet in the air. She distributed what plain liquids she had in the pack she'd grabbed, giving Red the only other energy drink. She needed him to be at his best or none of them might survive.

Trever curled his lip at the small packet she handed him. "Water? Hardly my usual choice of beverage."

"Fugitives can't be choosers," she said, twisting the old adage in an attempt to lighten the mood.

"Next time you escape a burning building, grab the feelgoods, would you?" The businessman drank his serving in a single gulp and handed her the empty container. Meg couldn't decide if he was joking or not.

"It's getting dark," Callina said, craning her neck to peer through the leafy canopy far above them. "Are we going to sleep here, in the branches?" Her husband rubbed her shoulders and guzzled the juice Meg had handed him.

"I want to get a little further to the west today, but yes, we're going to camp in the air." Red's tone was decisive. "Even if the Shemdylann find us, it'll be hard for them to recapture us. We can scatter along the branches. When I reconnoitered, the enemy hadn't made much more than a token effort at a ground search. Their beach party was going full steam, more raucous if anything, in alien style. I guess shore leave matters more to them than a few escaped prisoners at the moment."

"I'm surprised they haven't flown over, done scans, something," Meg said.

"Their inattention to escapees works in our favor. Five more minutes and then we move." Finishing his drink, Red crushed the packet and stuck it in his pocket. "Don't leave anything behind to provide a trail for the enemy in case someone higher up issues orders to venture deeper into the forest, tracking us."

Eyes wide, Bettis stopped in the act of crumpling the container in his hand. "Oh, yeah, of course. Good precaution."

"I dropped mine already," his wife said, eyes downcast and shoulders hunched, as if afraid of what Red might say or do.

"Can't be helped now," Meg said hastily. "Please be more careful from now on."

"Our survival is going to depend on how much the Shemdylann commander's personal honor is invested in losing us," Red said. "The big money for him is the ransom Finchon's going to pay. How many times did you hear him say we're not worth much?"

"He said you were," Callina pointed out.

"That's why the pirates took poor Harelly to feed the eels instead of you," Bettis said.

"Yeah, I'd forgotten, the enemy passed right over you." Trever spun on his heel and rejoined them. "What makes you so special, Third Officer Thomsill? Something we should all know perhaps?"

"Maybe the Shemdylann like tattoos." Eyes narrowed, Red gave him a hard stare, and the man subsided. "I guarantee you I'm not worth a massive effort to find us in this place." He gestured at the trees. "And I suspect the foliage may block the enemy scanners to some extent, if our pursuers do a cursory search. These trees must absorb quite a few trace minerals. Root systems are usually two to three times the size of the tree's crown, so the circulation in the trunk will draw nutrients from deep in the soil. I've seen the botanical mechanism before on other worlds."

"Dantaralon has troops of arboreal mammals," Meg added, recalling bits and pieces of the rangers' briefings on previous stops on this world. "We just haven't met any. Better hope we don't, as the primates can be fierce in a pack. Of course, enough of them might confuse the alien scanners too. Oh, and did I mention there are some gigantic tree snakes, by the way?"

"Better and better." Callina shivered. "Can we get going now?"

By the time Red signaled a halt for the night, visibility was limited. It might only be sunset above the trees, but under the dense canopy, the light cut out sooner. Meg came to a place where a tree had branched into two massive, joined trunks and there was extra space where the branches met the trunk. "How about here?" she said. "Plenty of room."

"Fine. Any restless sleepers in the bunch?" Red asked.

Meg wasn't surprised when Mrs. Bettis raised her hand. Red retraced his footsteps along the last branch he'd traversed and returned with some vines he'd slashed free with the knife Meg had salvaged from the ranger station. He handed some to Bettis. "Here, lash yourselves together."

The five of them sat, close together for warmth, Red in the middle, with Meg curled under his right arm and the Bettises on the other side. Trever maintained his distance from them, and still there was quite a bit of room on their makeshift platform. Meg did a quick survey of the remaining food in her pack and set half aside for tomorrow. She gave Red a double serving, telling him as he protested, "We need you to be at full strength, so eat. That's an order."

He subsided, grumbling but with a grin. She saw him tuck some of the food into his pants pocket, but she chose not to say anything. He knew what he needed and what he could do without. "We have a full day of travel tomorrow, and by midafternoon the day after we should arrive at the research station," he said. "I'm not expecting much there besides shelter. The scientists probably didn't leave anything behind, especially since the place shut down a few years ago, before whatever caused this crisis we're stuck in. I'm assuming the owners left in an orderly fashion. So, no cache of goodies. But if I can get the systems activated, we might be able to call for extraction. And the place appeared pretty well built on the maps, a lot of it below ground, so even if the Shemdylann find us somehow, burning us out won't be an option for them."

Lower lip quivering, Callina appeared to be counting the noodles in her small serving. "If the people who were working there took all their equipment and food, what are we going to eat? How will we survive?"

"Dantaralon is a lush planet," Meg said. "We can forage for nuts and berries once we're on the ground."

"There are small mammals to hunt," Red added. "I bet tree snake is pretty tasty if you cook it right."

Thinking about how helpless she'd been while the one crawled over her at the burned-out ranger station, Meg repressed a shudder. *But if I get hungry enough, I probably could eat it.* "We've had survival training," she said, indicating Red and herself. "We'll manage." Of course, her survival training had been one day in the middle of general cruise readiness training, but the lessons had come back to her pretty handily over the past forty eight hours. And she was sure Red could have been marooned anywhere with absolutely no resources and emerged unscathed, given his military training.

"So, you're telling me it's an adventure." Eyebrows raised, Callina seemed dubious.

"That's one way to think about the situation," Trever agreed, his tone sour.

Although it grew dark, Meg was surprised how much moonlight filtered through the leaves. Of course, Dantaralon did have four moons. Small iridescent insects flitted over their heads, the buzzing an annoyance once the novelty of the pretty glow wore off. The Bettises talked between themselves quietly for a bit and then settled to sleep. Trever continued his pattern of keeping pretty much to himself and was soon snoring on the edge of the group. Fortunately, his noise blended in with the calls of the night creatures.

Curled against Red's reassuringly warm bulk, Meg could tell he was awake. Although his breathing was even, his muscles were tense, as if he was poised for action. "I can split the night watch with you," she whispered. "You need sleep too."

"I'll be fine, cat naps, remember?" His voice held a hint of amusement. Then his tone dropped into a serious register. "Meg?"

"Yes?"

"I'm sorry I couldn't reach you, there in the cabin, when it was on fire. I was going to regret my failure to my dying day."

She patted his hand and then curled her fingers around his. "I survived. You rescued Callina; that's not trivial."

He hugged her closer to him and dropped a kiss on the top of her head. "I've been wondering all day—how did you get out?"

She told him a brief version of her escape, omitting the utter terror.

When she was finished with her bare bones recitation, he was silent for a moment, rubbing his thumb across her hand, before asking a new question. "What made you think of taking to the trees?"

"I grew up on a frontier planet in Sector Forty, with four older brothers. Climbing trees is one of the ways we spent our time when we weren't in school. Or in detention." She chuckled at the memories, keeping her mirth quiet, mindful of their sleeping passengers. Since he seemed to be in the mood to talk, she decided to probe a bit at his personal history. "What about you, any brothers or sisters?"

Stretching to unkink his back and then settling against the tree trunk, pulling her close, he grinned. "Yeah, I'm the youngest of six brothers. We homesteaded on the frontier as well. Most of us guys on my homeworld joined the military when we were old enough. The war with the Mawreg is a lot more real out there than it is to the Inner Sectors, I think."

"It was real to us on my planet. We had shelters and drills and a lot of military presence." She considered for a moment. "I rarely hear anything about the war nowadays, at least not while on a cruise. Of course, our passengers are trying to escape reality or they wouldn't be sailing with us. What made you decide to join the Special Forces?"

"Some of the more specialized branches of the military recruit for frontier kids. Our kind of survival skills are at a premium, and difficult to teach to soft Inner Sectors cadets." He nudged her gently in the ribs. "If you're not going to sleep, turnabout is fair play tonight—how did you follow a career path that brought you to a staff position on a luxury charter in the mid Sectors?"

"I should ask you how you became crew on the same boat," she said. "Not much to tell about me, you know as well as I do there aren't too many ways off a frontier world other than the military. I didn't want to live and die on one planet. I didn't see myself as a soldier, present circumstances excepted. One of my mother's cousins was pretty high in the Guild and she pulled strings to get me into training. I flew the outer runs, then immigrant ships, then cryo passenger vessels with a few cabins, and finally worked my way into charter."

"You ever think of signing on with one of the big lines, or an intermediate like CLC?"

She bit her lip. Now he was talking about her impossible dream. "Who hasn't? I've heard CLC's about the best for crew, since the SMT line went bankrupt. CLC pays a fair salary; you're not just living on tips. And the working conditions would be so much better. Our captain on the *Far Horizons* is—was—a pretty decent man, but you're at the mercy of the draw who you ship out with on these short charters. Can't refuse a berth, not more than once or twice. Guild frowns on exercising your options, no matter what the fine print says about crew rights. But the competition for the big liner slots is fierce."

"I have a berth waiting for me, working Security on a top of the line CLC cruiser, the *Nebula Princess*. We survive this dilemma, we're in; I can get you hired on."

She craned her neck to stare at him. "If you have a position with CLC, why are you wasting time crewing for this small outfit?"

She thought he wasn't going to answer because he was silent for so long. She turned to watch a pair of nocturnal winged insects wafting by on the breeze, wishing he would say more, explain himself.

Red took a deep breath. "Well, I met a girl and she works for this charter company. And I can't get her out of my mind, you see."

Meg turned to him and found him staring at her in the moonlight, eyes gleaming. She couldn't look away as he lowered his head, closing her eyes only as their lips met. His tongue swept the seam of her lips, and she parted them to grant him entry. But when Meg adjusted to make the embrace less awkward, looping her arm around Red's neck, Callina murmured in her sleep, stretching a bit.

Red broke off the kiss reluctantly, but continued to hold her close against him. She could hear his heart beating—a steady, reassuring sound in this tropical forest full of noisy night creatures. "Just tell me you don't hate the idea," he whispered, lips close to her ear. "Please."

"Idea?" Caught in the emotion of the moment, she wasn't sure if he was talking about working together for the CLC Line or referring to the attraction blossoming between them in this unlikely time and place.

"Us. Us together, anywhere you want to be," he said, as if reading her confusion.

"No, I-I don't hate the idea." Hand on the back of his head, threaded in the incredible softness of his hair, she guided him to an angle where their lips met in a quick kiss. Regretting this wasn't the time or place to explore the intriguing possibilities flooding through her mind, Meg ended the embrace all too soon. Survival was the top priority. "You get me the interview, and I'll do the rest on my own merits, though," she said, poking him in the chest with one finger.

He laughed. "I've no doubts."

CHAPTER FIVE

When she woke in the morning, Red was nowhere to be seen, but there were two huge, bowl-shaped green leaves filled with water sitting a short distance away on the branch. Yawning and stretching, she eyed her companions. "Did anyone see where Mr. Thomsill went?"

The others shook their heads or gazed at her in sleepy confusion. As she was becoming concerned about him, Red climbed onto the branch from below, her pack, now full of berries, looped over one of his broad shoulders.

"You took the risk of going down there?" she asked, pointing at the forest floor so far below.

He nodded. "Gathered dew for you first, before I descended to check for enemy activity. As long as I was on the ground reconnoitering anyway, decided I'd pick some berries. We're about out of food, right?"

"How do we know these are safe to eat?" Leaning over her husband's shoulder to see the offering better as Red set the bulging pack on the branch, Callina was dubious.

"All kinds of small mammals were eating them and one large bearlike creature. I had to find my own patch, wasn't going to fight him for breakfast. Must have outweighed me by two hundred pounds." Red popped several of the sapphire blue berries in his mouth, chewed and swallowed with enthusiasm. "I've already had quite a few and you don't see me keeling over."

Callina helped herself with no further hesitation, making a pouch with the skirt of her sundress and pouring several handfuls into the makeshift bowl.

Meg said, "Generally, most things on the planet are edible for humans. It's the wildlife that tends to be poisonous here." The berries had a delightful tang to them and the fiber of the seeds and skins was filling. "Any sign of pursuit?" Meg asked, going for her third helping after a refreshing swallow of the cold morning condensation he'd collected.

Tossing a berry high into the air and catching between his teeth, Red shook his head. "But we need to remain on high alert. It's fortunate the forest grows in the direction we want to go."

"I think the trees cover pretty much all of this continent," Meg said.

"If we stay marooned forever, maybe we can start a tree-dwelling civilization." Callina's voice held undeniable sarcasm.

A few minutes later, the group resumed hiking along the branches like veterans, traveling as directly west as possible. At times, a detour was required, climbing or descending to reach main branches growing in the correct heading, but overall progress was steady. Despite Red's warning earlier, Meg was relaxed and concentrating on the uneven bark under her feet when something large, making no sound other than a low hum, soared overhead. Above the treetops, the craft blocked the sun.

"Get to the nearest trunk and stay down," Red ordered.

Meg grabbed Callina and hustled to do as he wanted. Red joined them a moment later. Mr. Bettis huddled close to the tree that Meg and his wife had just traveled from. Trever put his back to a tree trunk and closed his eyes, hands clenched on protuberances in the bark, as if he was afraid a tractor beam was going to sweep the area and pull him into captivity.

"A Shemdylann ship?" Meg whispered, as the flyer lazily passed from view to the east. "Will they find us?"

"I hope not." Red kept scanning the sky. "I hope he's merely doing a few sweeps to say he made an effort."

The five humans stayed motionless for a good ten minutes by Meg's chrono, and when the enemy ship didn't return, continued on their journey.

At times, Meg thought this would have made a superb nature tour, worth as many credits as a visit to the Falls. The route took them through gorgeous areas of flowering vines, with jewel-like insects flitting in and out of the blooms. From a distance, Meg saw several small troops of the monkeylike climbers, grooming, eating, and sleeping. A few sentinel animals bared fangs at them, but apparently the humans were far enough away—or Red was imposing enough—preventing the creatures from initiating a territorial fight. Red hustled them through those areas as fast as he dared. Here and there a tree snake was coiled, the gorgeously tinted menace hugging its chosen branch. Meg insisted on sidetracking far out of their way to avoid any proximity to the snakes.

Red offered to kill one and cook it for lunch and she shuddered, clutching her stomach. "I'm not that desperate yet, thank you."

A flight of red and yellow song birds with long tails swooped over the branch, startling them so much Callina slipped and nearly fell before Red grabbed her arm.

The deeper Meg traveled into the forest, the more astounded she was by the quantity and beauty of the winged residents. All sizes and types of birds appeared to inhabit the area, from tiny jeweled sap drinkers to giant birds of prey with twelve foot wingspans, drifting on the air currents among the trees.

When Red called a halt for a midmorning break, he picked a spot close to a spectacular blanket of purple flowers growing on a nearby tree, cascading toward the ground, anchored by stout roots dug deep into the living tree. There were all types of birds drinking the nectar or hunting the lacy-winged insects hovering amid the blooms. The volume of bird songs was amazing. One of the red and yellow songsters flew to a small branch above them and trilled a crystalline run of notes.

Callina cleared her throat, stood and launched into a song in her bell-like soprano, more beautiful than Meg had ever heard from a human, not even on opera trideos of famous Inner Sector singers. Although Meg was far from being an expert on music, Mrs. Bettis had a range of at least three octaves. The song soared so high Meg's pulse pounded, and then there was an astonishing run of phrases, the pitch constantly changing to delight the ear, but sung at full volume. She glanced at Red, worried he might object to the unnecessary sound, but he gave every sign of enjoying the unusual performance. By the time their fellow refugee had finished her aria, with lingering notes, the closest branches were filled with songbirds of all colors and descriptions, heads tilted as the flock absorbed the concert. The humans applauded and Mr. Bettis gave his wife a kiss.

She curtseyed to the birds, who rose in a wave of noisy, kaleidoscopic colors, swirling through the nearby branches and going about their normal business.

"Amazing," Meg said. "Where did you learn to sing so beautifully?"

The passenger blushed. "I was in training at the Sector Fine Arts Academy because my stepfather had finally agreed that my voice was good enough to merit professional training." She had a rueful smile. "I was an asset, you understand? I entertained at some of his charity galas—he supported the school with scholarships. And paid my tuition, of course. I met Peter while we were making the arrangements for the various charity events and the concerts, and well, one thing led to another. This cruise was supposed to be our delayed honeymoon."

"I'm a lucky man." Mr. Bettis straightened his back and raised his chin.

"Not to dampen the mood—because I enjoyed the song as much as the birds did," said Red. "A rare treat. But we need to move out. Save your breath, Ma'am, and perhaps you can sing us a concert once we're safe at the research facility."

"Of course." Basking in their praise, Callina was as happy as Meg had ever seen her.

Twice more that morning, however, the sky darkened overhead and the Shemdylann shuttle made another pass in their area.

"This isn't good," Red said. "I think they're reading something on their scanners here, despite interference from the vegetation. We're probably lucky Crxtahl is sailing under direct orders from the Mawreg overlords. His bosses won't want him to linger on this planet, and won't appreciate him scorching the forest to ash, wasting armament trying to swat flies with a flame thrower."

Meg stared at him. "Would the Shemdylann destroy the rain forest? Just to keep the five of us from escaping?"

"In a heartbeat." Eyebrows raised, Red seemed surprised at her astonishment. "Intergalactic war isn't a game. It's played for keeps on a grand scale. We've burned off entire planets and so has the other side. And I'm afraid the commander's considerable ego is involved, since he's got a ship searching for us. Shemdylann attain and keep rank through ruthless success, and defeating constant challenges from ambitious subordinates. He can't afford to be seen as weak. I was hoping he'd be smart enough to deflect criticism from his troops for losing us, but when were the Shemdylann ever big thinkers?"

Wondering if she'd ever find out more about the experiences he'd endured in his years of service, she said nothing. He seemed so well versed on the enemy.

"You four stay here and be ready to move when I say so." Drawing the blaster, Red ran at full speed in the direction they'd come.

"What's he doing?" Callina asked.

"I have no idea." Meg was as puzzled as the others, but she was grateful for a chance to rest.

Moments later, a terrible shrieking filled the air, coming from the same direction Red had gone. At the same moment, the Shemdylann ship drifted by for the fourth time, close to the treetops, which were another hundred feet or so above Meg's head. She cringed, as if making herself smaller would save her from detection by the enemy. The noise in the trees came closer and she worried about what kind of threat might be approaching. Hands over her ears to block the yelling, which seemed to be from a large number of creatures, she hunkered down.

"Shouldn't we get out of here?" Mr. Bettis shouted, arms locked around his terrified wife. "Whatever's moving this way sounds worse than the Shemdylann. And the threat is here in the trees with us right this minute."

Meg shook her head. "Red said to wait here."

"You're in command, not him," Bettis said, pointing his finger at her.

She glared until he averted his eyes. "And I trust his combat skills. Stay here as ordered."

"Fuck this, you fools can wait here to see what's about to overrun us, I'm moving out." Trever sprinted away from them, running full tilt along a sturdy branch. "Every man for himself today."

Frustrated, Meg turned away. She couldn't abandon the others to chase him. He'd made his choice, and she hoped he wouldn't regret it.

Mouth open in surprise, Callina stood, pointing. "Lords of Space, it's some sort of stampede."

A troop of the tree-dwelling mammals was running along the branches and swinging on vines through the open spaces. The screaming and yelling came from the fleeing animals, green-blue fur on end and curly striped tails spiraled close to their bodies. Ears flat against their skulls, fangs bared, the troop of enraged beasts came in a wave.

Meg shrank back, pulling Callina with her. She realized Red was driving the creatures, using carefully aimed, short blasts from the blaster. He was hitting branches in close proximity to the troop to speed the laggards' progress and head the leaders in the direction he wanted. As the flood of angry animals reached the next tree trunk to the east, Red spaced his shots to force the alpha to climb instead of continuing on to where Meg and the others waited. Standing directly below the chittering, complaining animals, he whipped them into a frenzy with a few more well-placed shots at the heels of the rearguard climbing toward the crown of the tree. Meg heard the engines of the Shemdylann ship again.

"Run!" Red yelled, not taking his eyes off the animals. He fired a few more blasts to keep them motivated, and sprinted after Meg.

"The tree climbers'll emerge from the foliage right under the ship's scanners," he said, running so easily right on her heels that she was jealous of his stamina. "I'm betting the pirates will be fooled into thinking they've been tracking the animals all this time. Worth wasting some blaster charge if we can decoy the enemy away."

"Clever. We're tree climbing mammals too," she said.

"Exactly." He took her elbow to help her navigate a huge knothole in the branch she was travelling. "Shemdylann scanners aren't well calibrated. Or at least the tech wasn't up to par last time I was on an operation downrange."

Meg stopped with a shriek as something heavy hit the branch right in front of her. She realized a heartbeat later it was Trever, sprawled across the wood like a broken doll. Red moved in front of her and knelt by the body. "I wondered where he'd gone."

"He refused to wait with us when you were driving the animals in our direction," Meg said.

Red had his fingers pressed to Trever's neck. "He's dead."

Retreating a step, hand to her mouth, Meg said "Did the pirates kill him somehow?"

Aiming the blaster at the body, Red fired a short burst of low intensity fire at something on the dead man's arm. "Spiders!"

Callina shrieked as a cluster of fist-sized, yellow-and-black arachnids scuttled away from Trever's corpse, scattering along the branch and taking shelter in nearby nooks and crannies of the bark. Meg yanked her backpack off and swiped at a particularly large specimen crawling in her direction, dropping bag and spider into the two hundred foot void below the branch. Shuddering, she followed the passengers to the tree they'd left, where the three of them huddled close to the reassuring bulk of the trunk for a moment. More slowly, Red joined them, scanning the branch as he came.

"How do you suppose Trever tangled with those?" Meg asked.

"He was always careless about tearing through the hanging vines growing in our path, rather than detouring," Red said. "I untangled him more than once, remember? He just wanted to bull through them or any other obstacle like he did to the human opponents in his playing days. We've seen a lot of insects, so I'm betting the spiders live in the foliage as well. He must have disturbed a nest."

"And like everything native to Dantaralon, the spiders are evidently poisonous." Callina gave the nearest cascade of brightly colored flowers draped over a nearby branch a nervous glance, edging closer to her husband.

"What are you going to do with the—with Trever?" Bettis asked. "We can't leave him here."

"I don't have time for burial detail, nor am I about to carry a corpse hundreds of feet to the ground. We leave him." Red's tone was uncompromising. "I'm concerned about saving the living while we still have time."

"Some ancient cultures arranged their dead in trees or on platforms," Callina said unexpectedly. "To be closer to the Lords of Space." As the others swung to give her their attention, she added, "Or whoever their deity was."

Meg seized on the idea. "If we can cover him with small branches maybe? And say a few words? Then it won't be so harsh, just…walking away."

Red grumbled, but obliged her by moving Trever's body to lie against the nearest trunk, and then took her knife to slash small branches in the vicinity, which the others piled in a fragrant mound over their late companion. Meg commended his spirit to the keeping of the Lords of Space and Red had them on the move again as soon as she uttered the final words.

Callina didn't offer to sing.

Red steered them north for about an hour before correcting their course to the westerly heading again. It seemed his stratagem had worked, because they didn't see the Shemdylann shuttle, which was a relief.

But relief never lasted too long on this voyage, Meg reflected, while resting during a lunch break. "Am I seeing things, or is it getting dark early today?"

"Kinda windy too," Callina said. "Worse than yesterday, anyhow."

Meg and Callina exclaimed in unison, "Storm!" Meg grabbed Red's arm. "How many cells were you and Drewson tracking when we landed?"

"Two, with a third one beginning the process of coalescing around an eye." He stood, tilting his head in an effort to peer through the canopy of leaves and branches above them. "I think I see clouds. Guess I'd better shinny a bit higher and verify. You keep walking. I'll be along soon."

Meg took him aside as the Bettis couple scrambled to identify the next branch and hike per orders. "If there's a storm brewing like the one we had at the ranger station, how are we going to shelter?" She stared at the forest surrounding them. "We'll never make it here. The wind must howl through these branches. And the last storm took down a tree as big as these. Would conditions ground level be any better? Should we descend for the night?"

"One problem at a time. First, let me see if there is a weather threat." Brow furrowed, eyes narrowed, he climbed to the next higher branch and kept going.

All too soon, he rejoined them, dropping on the branch in front of Meg like a big cat. "Major storm on the way all right. The front is blowing in fast."

"Can we tie ourselves together with the vines? Maybe lash ourselves to a tree?" Mr. Bettis asked.

"We could, but keeping ourselves from blowing away in the gale wouldn't solve the problem of the rain. At these wind speeds, the droplets will hit like projectiles." Red frowned at Callina's sundress over a swimsuit. "We're not exactly dressed for a storm."

"Let's keep moving, see if we come across anything we can use for shelter, maybe a hollow tree or dense branches, perhaps closer to the ground," Meg said. "The first thing we find, we settle in."

"Agreed. I'll scout ahead." Red was off, moving faster than Meg would have dared, supremely confident of his balance.

She led the two passengers after him at a more deliberate pace. The breeze was definitely picking up, buffeting her from odd directions as she hiked along the branches.

Then Red was there, broad grin on his face. "You won't believe what I've found for shelter."

Half annoyed, Meg was astounded at his amusement, given their tight situation, caught in the open with a storm about to pummel them any minute. "What?"

His expression grew even more mischievous. "Oh, no, you have to see it to believe it. But the entrance is tricky, so we need to hurry before the winds intensify."

A few moments later he brought them to a halt where one of the giant trees had forked into three trunks. Built securely into the fork was an odd structure, like a small hut, maybe fifteen feet across and five feet high, made of woven twigs, dried mud, and other materials. The breeze pushing at her didn't so much as stir the dwelling.

Meg examined the odd construction from various angles, holding her hair out of her face with difficulty. "Is it a nest of some sort?"

Red nodded. "Probably built by those birds of prey. Remember the ones gliding on the thermals above us yesterday? The nest is big enough to accommodate their wingspan."

Her memory crystal clear on the menacing knifelike talons and beaks on the largest birds she'd seen, Meg was concerned. "Won't the current owners be upset at us moving in?"

"I've checked it out already. Either the nest was never occupied or else it's been abandoned for a long time. It's clean, not even feathers, no sign of previous tenants."

"I'm not riding out a storm like the one we had before in some bird's nest," said Callina, eyebrows raised to her hairline. "Are you crazy?"

"It's obviously been here a long time and survived many a storm intact," Red informed her. "Unless the tree falls, we'll be fine. The birds or whoever built this thing anchored it to the tree with mud and vines. The mud dried to a stone-like consistency and the vines have taken root in the tree itself. Clever construction—never underestimate Mother Nature's ingenuity. There's nowhere else and we've got to get under cover in the next few minutes." He appealed to Meg.

She grabbed at Callina as a stray gust threatened to knock the woman off her feet. "Yes, fine, where's the entrance?"

"You have to climb to the narrow branch, right below." He pointed. "Then up into the nest," he said. "I'm guessing the design of the entrance is a defense against the tree snakes. The reptiles must like birds' eggs. There's a broad shelf inside where the eggs probably would have been, but it'll do as a resting place for us tonight."

Meg assessed Mrs. Bettis, who was white-faced and trembling with exhaustion. "We're not all as athletic as you are, Red."

"I'll go first and help haul each of you into the nest. Bettis, you follow me and one of us can stay on the perch to catch the women as each climbs across, while the other man pulls them to safety inside."

Meg insisted on being the last woman to make the transfer. She watched, heart pounding, as Callina made the tricky descent onto the smaller branch below the nest, which swayed in the rising wind and wasn't nearly as safe as the broader limbs they'd been traversing for two days. Then she pulled herself into the structure, disappearing from view. When Meg made the trip, she tried not to glance down. Red's strong arms locking around her brought relief as she was hauled to safety.

"Cramped quarters in here, but warm and dry," he said, as he held her close for a moment.

Red helped her into the spot he'd picked for her, with the Bettis couple on the other side.

She could hear the wind howling around the tree outside the nest, but it was cozy, their body heat soon warming the odd shelter. She doled out the nuts and berries Red had foraged during the day and the four of them sat in the gloom munching on the sparse meal. Torrents of rain blew by the nest's opening, but the interior remained dry.

"It's reasonable to expect this'll blow over in twelve hours, like the last storm did," Red said.

"Tomorrow we'll be at the research facility, and hopefully things will be much more civilized," she said.

"Can't get less civilized," Mr. Bettis answered from his position. "I'm not complaining," he added hastily.

"Adventure," his wife said with a shrug.

The tree shuddered under them as a particularly strong gust of wind roared through the area. Thunder boomed directly overhead. Meg grabbed at Red and stifled a shriek. He put his arm around her. "It'll be all right. There are a lot of other places for the lightning to hit besides here. Taller trees. We deserve a break." In the gloom, she could tell he was doing a double take. "Hey, are you okay? You're shaking like a leaf." His voice was soft, for her ears alone. "Cold?"

She was silent for a moment. "I have a thing about storms," she said finally.

"Seems to be a pretty bad 'thing'," he answered. "This is one of the few times you've displayed any nerves at all on this trek."

"I have nerves." She laughed. "You should have seen me quaking when I was searching for the courage to run from the ruined station into the forest with an unknown enemy lurking."

"But you infallibly do what needs to be done." Red's voice was admiring.

There was a violent flash of light and the explosive boom of thunder directly outside. Red held her close with one arm. Meg ran her fingers through her hair, gently combing the tangled tresses, the motion soothing.

"Do you want me to go outside and check the stability of the nest?" Red asked.

"No!" The idea gave Meg the chills. "Even with your size, you'd be blown away. I'm ordering you to stay inside."

He subsided. "I'd be happy to make the attempt, if it would give you peace of mind."

"And I appreciate the offer, but there'll probably be more close hits like that one and you can't investigate them all. Or do much about the wind damage either. I'll be fine." She realized he wouldn't press her for an answer about her aversion to storms. Red was proving himself to be an understanding person and perversely, his empathetic, no-questions attitude made her want to explain herself. She swallowed hard. "When I was five, I was playing hide-n-seek with my brothers. At some point, my siblings decided it would be funny to go home without bothering to find me." She made herself shrug, trying to make light of the incident—it was an old memory, but dredging it up still brought shivers to her spine. When she realized she'd been left alone, the terror had overwhelmed her younger self. Trying to keep a light tone, she continued. "Kids, you know? By the time I figured it out, it was getting dark and a massive thunderstorm hit. I spent the night in the woods. I don't even remember some of it. The doctors said it was disassociation. Anyway, storms combined with being in the woods are my worst nightmare."

"Didn't your parents search for you?" He sounded angry on behalf of her five-year-old self.

"Not until morning. There was a tornado warning, and no one was allowed out of the community shelter. My brothers never forgave themselves, but I've forgiven them."

"I'd have searched," he said, his voice quiet and sure. "I'll always find you, Meg."

She curled her hand around his and rested her head on the nest wall behind her. "You're a comforting person to have around, Simon Thomsill."

"Well, you say that *now*, Miss Antille, but until recently, I had the distinct impression I was more of a nuisance." His voice was teasing.

"Well, you are a rookie." Meg was amused at how much fun it was to tease him in return.

"Not at everything," he said. "I'm exceedingly good at some things. Which I hope to be able to prove to you at some point."

The wind howled and there was another cannonade of thunder. Red leaned over so he could speak close to her ear. "I screwed up whenever you were around," he admitted. "Fell over my own feet, as it were. Couldn't help myself. Drove me nuts, being so clumsy, which is not my normal operating mode, but you have quite the effect on me. Of course, Drewson and the others thought it was hilarious to steer me in the wrong direction, like with the coffee request on the shuttle the day we arrived here."

"I can't imagine elite soldiers fall over their own feet much," she said, hoping he could hear the teasing in her tone, over the storm's ruckus.

"Making a good impression on you mattered to me. You're important to me."

Closing her eyes for a moment, Meg indulged in some mental pictures of Red in short sleeves, muscles bulging, the hint of a tattoo on his upper arms, along with his smile and the warmth of his blue eyes. Knowing she was taking a step into vulnerable emotional territory for herself, she decided to pursue the topic. "Keeping my distance wasn't personal," she said. "I had a couple of bad experiences with crew when I first shipped out, being a naïve girl from a frontier planet, you know? Such a cliché, but true. I learned my lesson the hard way. Luxury yachts are too small when a crew-staff romance goes bad. Lost my first berth, nearly got a black mark on my record when the captain sided with his First Officer, rather than believe me. And after the case was over, I said I'd never get involved with another shipmate. Too complicated."

"Is your rule subject to negotiation?"

She answered his question with one of her own, something on her mind since he'd first mentioned the subject. "Did you mean what you said—you signed onto our ship because of me?"

"I dropped in on the Guild mixer on Sector Hub and you were there. The one celebrating the planet's First Ship Day? My buddy, the one who's hiring me for the CLC lines, talked me into going. I…had some pretty bad experiences on my last couple of missions, spent time in medical, wasn't fit for downrange duty any longer, according to the medicos. So I'm going civilian. He suggested that I mingle with my new peers."

Hearing bitterness in his voice, she squeezed his hand. "Hey, you're doing pretty damn good so far in this mess we're caught in."

"Praise from my commanding officer is not to be sneezed at." He kissed her hand. "Anyway, you were there, with a bunch of other staff and crew, and once I saw you, I couldn't stop staring."

Meg didn't know what to say, settling for murmuring, "I'm nothing special, Red."

"Sez you. I felt like I'd been hit by a comet when the crowd shifted and there you were." The wind rose to a shriek, cutting off the conversation for a few moments. When the volume outside became bearable again, Red continued. "Have you heard of the Mellureans?"

Wondering how the odd segue could be relevant, she said, "Yes, who hasn't? Telepathic, maybe shape-changing, an ancient race here long before the humans of Terra made it out into the galaxy. I always had half a suspicion the whole story was a myth. Or something invented by the trideo industry."

"Oh, they exist all right. We do protection duty sometimes in the Teams, if the person is high value enough. My unit got assigned as bodyguards to a Mind of Mellure once. Lady Jeffek, one of their ruling Council. I can't tell you anything about the circumstances, classified till I die. Ask me, we were window dressing, there to demonstrate the human commitment to the objective. Lady Jeffek was pure power and she had her own bodyguards besides. The whole delegation was spooky."

"What happened?" Fascinated by this view into an exotic legend, Meg couldn't imagine how the topic related to Red's pursuit of her.

"Enlisted bodyguards are most definitely *not* encouraged to chitchat with the sentient being protected. Hell, no one talks to a Mellurean without being invited to do so. I've heard even the Mawreg are afraid of Mellureans. That's what made the incident with me so odd. She and her retinue were leaving, the job was done, and we were about to stand down and redeploy. She—the Mind—stopped in front of me and never spoke a word, or so my buddies swore later. All I knew was she transfixed me with one look from her huge violet-blue eyes and I couldn't look away. It was like an out of body experience, paralysis or something. In my head, I heard a voice say 'You have one chance in your life at true love, Simon Thomsill. When the moment presents itself, promise me you'll pursue the chance. To lose true love is the saddest fate that can befall a being.' And then she'd walked on and I wasn't sure the whole thing wasn't a dream."

"She gave you a prophecy? Just *gave* you a prophecy? I've heard the Sectors' government begs for any scrap of help or advice from Mellure."

"Yeah, I know, hard to believe. The Mellureans rarely choose to interact with humans, much less tell fortunes. They have their own agenda, and from what I know, the Sectors try to stay out of their way and hope their objectives align with ours." He picked at a twig protruding from the nest floor, crumbling the attached dry leaves between his fingers. "I heard scuttlebutt later that if a Mellurean dies, his or her mate dies too, because the two beings are linked so tightly to each other on the mental plane. I don't know if it's true, but if her people take mating so seriously, the belief might explain why she took a moment to speak to me, give me a prophecy about love." He rubbed his head. "The higher ups didn't even ask me what she'd said. In fact, the general sent for me immediately and told me not to ever repeat what she'd communicated, not even to him, and to absolutely do whatever she'd told me. I saluted and said, 'Yes, sir'."

Meg tried to imagine someone speaking to her telepathically. "What did her voice sound like in your head?"

"You know that song Mrs. Bettis sang earlier?"

Meg nodded. "Gorgeous music."

"Lady Jeffek's voice sounded like music, only using words, not notes. Seeing you at the Guild party, I heard the echo of her voice, like she was standing next to me."

Meg knew her jaw dropped. "Why didn't you talk to me? Ask me to dance? Buy me a drink?" She pushed at his rock hard bicep. "And don't try to tell me you're shy."

"I wanted to approach you, but you were sitting there, surrounded by people you seemed to be friends with. And I watched the way you refused other guys. You were more of an observer than a participant. Your girlfriends were dancing with any male sentient who asked, but you sat there nursing your drink. I wanted to know what you were thinking; I wanted to talk to you all night—" He broke off, leaning his head against the nest. "She—the Mellurean—only said it was a chance. I was afraid to blow the chance. I had to get it right. Get to know you as a person, not merely have a dance and a drink."

Or a one night stand. Meg didn't say anything. She might have danced with him if he'd asked, but then again, maybe not. "I was in a pretty bad mood that night. Our tip for the last charter was shabby because the Third Officer messed up, made the Primary on the cruise angry, which is why we had a crew vacancy. I wasn't able to send my family the usual amount, and I know they needed it pretty badly, so I wasn't in the mood for company. Probably wise you steered clear."

"I asked the bartender if she knew you, or what line you worked for. She told me, and added the ship had a crew vacancy. I took the open crew slot as a sign. So I put my other job on hold and signed on. But you've got keeping your distance refined to an art form."

She snuggled close to him. "I was tempted to break my no fraternization rule when it came to you, more than once. I admit it."

"Really?" He sounded delighted.

"Yes. We're certainly getting to know each other now," Meg said.

"And?"

"And I like what I'm finding out." Meg's cheeks grew warm from blushing, but he wouldn't be able to tell in the gloom. "And we're marooned now, you know, not shipmates."

"I've thought of that," he admitted with a chuckle. "I'll take any loophole."

"I'm going to get some sleep now," she said. "The storm's dying down somewhat. Less wind."

"Have good dreams." He leaned over to kiss her cheek, but she turned so their lips met and the caress turned into quite an involved tangle of their tongues, arms awkwardly wrapped around each other, trying not to disturb the others. "Lords of Space, grant this research facility has stout defenses and some damn privacy," Red said as they drew apart.

CHAPTER SIX

"Bad news," Red said.

Meg and the others gathered around, sipping at the leaves full of dew she'd gathered.

"The idiots who built the research facility cleared the trees away on either side. We're going to have to cross open ground to get in."

"How much further is it?" Meg asked.

"Maybe half an hour at the speed you're going." Tilting the makeshift leaf cup to his lips, Red drank deeply of the water she handed to him.

"We haven't seen any Shemdylann ships since before the storm. Maybe the enemy abandoned the search," Meg said.

"I hope so." Wiping his lips, he said, "Either way, we'd better hike."

When she was standing at the last tree before the small man-made clearing where the research facility stood, Meg wasn't impressed with the place Red had driven them so hard to reach, and she hated the idea of leaving the sanctuary of the forest.

The research facility was unimpressive, not even as large as the ranger station. It was a brown and gray square building, with slab sides and an angular roof, featureless.

"How do we get in?"

"The entry is on the south side," Red said. "We'll have to circle around to it."

"There's no landing pad," Meg said. "Odd. How did they bring supplies and staff in and out?"

"One of many mysteries here," Red answered. "Once we get inside, I'm hoping to learn a lot more."

Staying close to Red, Meg led her other two companions clockwise through the edge of the trees, getting into position to face the entry. Eventually, after nearly circling the entire building, she was relieved to observe the usual control panel on an exterior wall. "What's our plan?"

"I'm going to open the door. I'll go in alone, check out the interior, and make sure it's safe for us. Then I'll signal for you three to hightail it while I provide what cover I can with the blaster."

Nodding her approval, Meg watched with clenched fists as he proceeded to carry out the steps he'd outlined. She alternated between watching Red work on the portal and scanning the sky for their enemy. A one person-sized gap appeared in the gray portal as he punched in his code, and Red stepped cautiously inside. She gasped, taking an involuntary step into the open as the door closed after him. Callina tugged on her shirttail to bring her into the cover of the forest. The next five minutes felt like an hour, until the door slid open again and Red reappeared, waving them on.

She gripped Callina's hand tight. "Ready?"

"I sure am," Mrs. Bettis said. "I've had enough of roughing it in the woods to last me a lifetime. Adventure has become a dirty word to me."

On Meg's count of three, she sprinted across the uneven ground, hoping the others were close behind. Mr. Bettis tripped on a root and fell headlong, his wife stopping to help him, screaming at him the whole time. Blaster at the ready, Red kept his eyes on the sky, which thankfully remained empty of Shemdylann, until Meg and Callina had moved past him into the safety of the facility. Then he ran to help Bettis get to his feet, looping the man's arm around his shoulder and half carrying him, limping, across the threshold.

The door snicked shut on their heels.

Hands at her waist, gasping for breath, Meg surveyed the room. "This is ridiculous. There's nothing here. It's some kind of reception area."

Bettis leaned on the wall, favoring his ankle and laughing.

In her present mood, Meg was easily irritated. "What's so funny?"

"PolyStarMed." Bettis pointed at the corporate symbol on the wall and emblazoned on the deserted desk.

Hands on her hips, Meg's irritation grew. "Yeah? So?"

"Finchon owns them. It's a minor holding through one of his shell companies."

"Small galaxy." Red shrugged.

"I wonder if he knew this was here?" Meg said.

"Doubtful." Bettis shook his head. "Even he doesn't know the infinite details of all his businesses. That's what he has me and a bunch of other flunkies for."

"I feel safer inside, though, whoever owns the business," Meg said. "This place seems much more of a fortress than the ranger station." She patted the solid wall beside her. "No windows to hurl fire bombs through. So, is the rest underground?"

Red nodded. "Makes sense when you consider the severity of the storms this planet suffers. I'd build down myself." He pointed at the far wall. "There's a gravlift."

"Is it working?" Despite being in a more secure situation, away from prying flyovers and scanners, Meg wasn't impressed so far. The facility appeared to offer nil in the way of resources. She almost believed she'd rather remain in the forest than this deserted place, but of course there wasn't any way to call for help in the open. And they might not be so lucky at finding sturdy shelter the next time a storm hit.

"The staff left all the systems fully powered and enabled, unlike the ranger station. I'm guessing the energy grid is a few decades more modern, integrated. Unless the building is demolished, the power is available until the core deteriorates. Takes centuries." Red waved a hand. "Notice the lights? Came on by themselves when I entered."

She realized she'd taken the diffused illumination for granted. Mood improving, she retrieved her backpack from the floor and said, "What are we waiting for? The sooner we make this place ours, the sooner we can call for a rescue."

Red activated the gravlift, standing aside with a bow. "After you."

One after the other Meg and the Bettis couple descended one level, stepping off in another brightly lit chamber. Five corridors stretched away on all sides, like spokes in a wheel.

"No one goes off exploring on their own," Red said. "It should be safe here, but I prefer to have all of you where I can see you for now, until we've scoped out the facility."

"Here's a map." Meg pointed at the display next to the gravlift and the others crowded to peer over her shoulder.

The research facility was five levels, plus the reception kiosk above. The first level, where she was standing, consisted of offices, a cafeteria with an attached kitchen, sickbay, a conference room, and the control room. The second level was living quarters, another tiny kitchen, a gym, and storerooms. The third level was labelled as lab space and storage, and the fourth bore the label "Controlled Access Only." A fifth level showed as "Sealed Building Systems."

"Probably not a good thing the fourth level is glowing red." Meg ran her finger across the lower segment of the map.

"We don't know. It could be a simple reminder it's a limited access space." Red didn't sound too hopeful. "I wish we could find out why the place was abandoned, though."

"If I had my AI, I could tell you," Bettis said. "It'd take some digging, because this was one tiny piece of Finchon's business, but I could have found out."

"But surely we're safe, right?" Callina rubbed her arms and stumbled away from the building map, going to the center of the open space. "I mean, whatever research was done here wasn't dangerous? To humans?"

"I think we're fine." Meg tried to be reassuring. "We've got no reason to descend to the fourth level. Red'll figure out the communications, call for help, and we'll be on our way home."

"Sure, simple." Red's calming tone was contradicted by the flat expression in his eyes, but Mrs. Bettis heaved a gasp of relief. "Here's something on the third level, an access tunnel maybe." He traced that part of the diagram across the map with his index finger, and a new portion of the wall came to life with flowing illumination. "There's the landing pad, maybe a quarter mile away."

"Why locate it over there?" Meg asked.

"Does it matter? Let's do a quick scan of this floor, see if any food or liquids were left in the kitchen or if I need to go hunting before dark. I need to see the control room too. Then we'll go down one level to the quarters and pick out rooms to call our own while we're here." Red stretched, unkinking his spine and rolling his shoulders. "It'll be nice to sleep in a real bed for a change, assuming the furniture was modular, built-in and not removed when the place was abandoned."

"Sounds good." Meg headed for the cafeteria, the others on her heels. The door opened as she approached and she stopped on the threshold so suddenly Callina bumped into her and sent her staggering a step or two. "What in the seven hells—"

The tables bore mute evidence to the previous inhabitants having been called away in the middle of a meal. Plates laden with moldy, desiccated food and stained, crusted cups sat at numerous places. The chairs were pushed away from the tables and several were overturned, as if their occupants had departed in haste.

"I thought you said this place was shut down in an orderly fashion?" Meg asked Red.

"Maybe the rangers didn't know the full story. Just that the installation went inactive." He moved around her into the room. "Even if there was a problem, the event was years ago. We're here now and the fact that the building is accessible argues the evacuation, or hasty exit or whatever happened, was precautionary. Let's see what's in the kitchen. I have hope for finding a hoard now."

The group walked through the small space single file, Callina setting chairs upright as she passed, as if she could restore normalcy.

The kitchen reminded Meg of the galley on the *Far Horizon*, efficient and compact. There was an area where individuals could reheat prepared food and a larger area where apparently a cook had worked on meals for the whole staff. A messy clump of gray mold showed where bread or fruit had been in a bowl. Pans on the stove held remnants of whatever had been in process on the day the place was abandoned. Ignoring the distasteful scraps, she walked to the cupboards, which opened easily under her touch, apparently not locked to any one person. "Oh, we're going to eat well tonight." She surveyed the stacks of sealed foodstuffs and did a little dance step. "It's a good omen."

"Dried fruit," Callina said with a happy laugh. "May I have some?"

"I think we'll all have some." Meg passed out the brightly colored packets of sweet dried fruits. "We need to celebrate reaching this place and getting safely inside," she said to Red, who had an impatient frown on his face. "Is the water running?"

He took the packet of Terran apricots she handed him and strolled to the double sink. Flipping the control one handed, he was rewarded by a gush of bubbling water. Meg tossed him a mug from the rack on the wall. After rinsing off the dust, he filled it to the brim, moving aside so Callina could get herself a drink.

"I crave a shower," Meg said. "Even if the hot water isn't running. My hair smells like smoke."

"I have leaves and twigs in mine." Callina tried to comb through her hair with her fingers.

Red flicked another tab and the water instantly changed to steaming hot. "I'd say we're good. Why don't you stay here and enjoy the refreshments, and I'll check out the rest of this level. Then we can all go to the next level and see what the conditions are in the living area."

"Sounds like a plan." Meg was opening more storage units, Callina right behind her.

Red helped Mr. Bettis limp to the nearest chair, at a clean table, and then he returned to the central area, presumably to carry out his plan of reconnoitering the rest of the level.

Blaster in hand, although there was precious little charge remaining, Red prowled through Level One, finishing his exploration in the control room, which was his desired destination. Despite his putting a good face on it for Meg and the others, unease kept pricking his nerves. The mess in the cafeteria hinted at some major problem having caused the abandonment of the place, and the flashing red indicators for Level Four were also unsettling.

The control chamber showed few signs of the hasty exit. There was a security desk, with currently blank monitors. Red scanned the labels and realized from here he could check out every room in the place except the private quarters on Level Two. He rested one hand on the chair, but paused before sitting. Moving to the next console, which appeared to be communications, he nodded in satisfaction.

Choosing to sit here, he activated the unit, silently blessing whoever had decided to leave the power grid active. *Might even write them a thank you note, once we're safely out of here.*

He tried the planetary links first, not surprised to find only silence. Other than the now destroyed ranger station, there was no other known outpost on Dantaralon. Then he switched to the internal link between this installation and the landing field a quarter of a mile away, at the end of the service tunnel. Again, nothing but a hum from the equipment.

Next, he opened the channels for offworld. Harsh Shemdylann voices spilled into the room and hastily he thumbed the volume down. Listening to their chatter ship to ship for a while, he heard no mention of his own party. The enemy forces were running through some kind of drill, maybe in preparation for the future attack on Sector Hub the heedless sentry had told him about on the beach. He chuckled as he listened to the ships' captains cursing at each other. Shemdylann didn't play nice amongst themselves. Interesting the Mawreg had sent this set of clowns to soften up Sector Thirty. A half a dozen scenarios to explain the strategy flooded his mind and angrily he muted the com volume.

You're not on active duty anymore; it's not your job to play war games. It's your job to get Meg and the others rescued.

Shaking off the remnants of his old military mindset, he started searching the intergalactic channels, but found no human transmissions. He hadn't expected any. Clearly, this area was under a warn-off that somehow had escaped the attention of the *Far Horizon's* captain, or else the charter had been overlooked by Sector authorities. Either way, someone screwed up badly, letting a passenger vessel wander into a war zone.

Okay, time to get into the military channels. For the only time in his life, he wished he'd been one of the guys picked for the fastlink experimental gear, to be able to send message from anywhere, anytime. Although rumor was, each time the link was activated, the operator took a year off his or her life. He'd make that sacrifice gladly if it meant he could get Meg to safety sooner.

The communications unit was locked out of military channels. He'd expected as much, but since the equipment was a standard unit from a major manufacturer, Red knew it had the capability to access the network. This wasn't his area of expertise—he'd had a bit of training on it along the way, so it took Red time to figure out how to work around the control. He tried various overrides and workarounds until suddenly a new set of indicators glowed green. "Gotcha!" He relied on the code his unit used the last time he was downrange, knowing it probably wouldn't be current, but all he wanted was to draw attention. Someone sending Special Forces code from a planet deep in a war zone should raise red flags. The only questions in his mind were how long would it take to evoke a response, and could he persuade Command to authorize an extraction?

Drumming his fingers on the edge of the console, he considered what to send. The message had to be short but pithy. He settled for "Extraction needed, 3 civilians and self," signed it with his service number and added the code for this general area of the Sector. Once encrypted, he sent the message, setting the system to resend the data at irregular intervals. No use drawing the Shemdylann attention. While he was waiting to see what kind of response he was going to get, if any, he moved to the Security desk. First, he activated the outside scanners, since he definitely wanted to be warned if anyone approached, and then he worked his way through the other floors of the installation. The place was empty, although as with the cafeteria, each area showed signs of an emergency evacuation.

He was about to activate the monitors on Level 4 when he heard a ping from the com desk. "Pretty fast response time."

Receiving a reply so soon meant there had to be a ship or a unit operating not too far away. His hopes rose the tiniest bit.

When he checked the received queue, a single word blinked at him. "Identify."

Fair enough. He punched his serial number in again, only to receive another laconic reply, "Proof?"

There was a counter code for authentication, but of course it was as out of date as anything else he could access. He typed the symbols and sent them on their way. The response arrived quickly and was longer.

"If you are who you say you are, what in the seven hells are you doing outside the fence?"

"Long story." Fingers flying on the keyboard, he added sparse details. "Cruise gone wrong. Have intel."

There was no response for a nerve-racking few minutes. He occupied himself watching the exterior monitors, where a family of the bearlike animals was wandering by.

The next transmission was a voice he hadn't heard for quite a few years. "Who the hell are you and how did you end up in the middle of all the tangos?"

"I know we're in a bad spot, Max," he said. "I need extraction and I need it three days ago."

"Oh, you think you know me, do you? Can you prove it?" The voice wasn't hostile, just flat and disinterested.

"Shall we talk about shore leave on Mirkessa Twelve? Remember what you got tattooed on a very private place?" There was silence from the other end. "Want me to specify on an open channel? Your old lady like it when you got home?" Despite the dicey circumstances he was currently mired in, Red's memories of the wild, drunken night after the successful conclusion of a tense mission were vivid and amusing.

"Stand down, soldier, don't reveal classified details." The laconic voice had a hint of a laugh now, but the next words were deadly serious. "No can do on pickup. The whole area is hot. Best you go to ground, wait things out. Maybe we can send a drone to do a supply drop."

Out of the corner of his eye, Red saw Meg enter the room, preceded by the smell of delicious coffee and hot food. He lifted a hand to acknowledge her presence, but kept his focus on persuading his old friend to do what he wanted. "If it was me alone, no problem. Inconvenient, but I could dance with the enemy for years and not get caught. You know that. I got two women and one injured civvie here. I've also got intel on the tangos' plans."

"Yeah, I heard you the first time on the intel. Sorry, your party is your problem. Command'll never give clearance—"

Meg stifled a gasp behind him.

Red cut into Max's apology. "Hey, the authorities screwed up, letting this cruise charter into the area in the first place, and they know it by now. Somebody with gravity *owes* these people."

There was silence for a moment. Then, "You sound pretty invested."

Red clenched his jaw, about to play his final card. He hoped it was a supernova. "Remember the guard duty we pulled for that Mellurean Mind, on Twigran Seven? Ten years ago?"

Max whistled. "Shit, this predicament you're in has to do with the Mellurean prophecy?"

Red turned, watching the play of emotions on Meg's face, wishing he knew what she was thinking. Frustration over his inability to accomplish her rescue this minute burned in his gut. Stretching a point about what the Mind had told him years ago, he clenched his jaw and said, "Yes." It wasn't like anyone was going to check with Lady Jeffek.

"Give me twelve. Out." There was a burst of sound as the link was cut off from the other end.

"The military don't want to rescue us, do they?" Meg didn't sound surprised.

He eyed her curiously as he took the coffee she handed over. "No. I think this entire system is flooded with Shemdylann, maybe this whole end of the Sector. Extraction will be risky."

Perching on the edge of the console, hands folded in her lap, she gave him a level stare. "We could do what he said, dig in and wait. Hide."

"You're calm about the prospect."

She arranged his dinner on the desk near his elbow. "I was a kid growing up on a frontier world, remember? Good survival skills. You and I could take care of the others. Even if we didn't dare stay at this facility too long, we could manage. I hate for anyone to risk themselves trying to rescue us if the situation is so dire." Meg focused on the blinking lights on the com console, unshed tears making her eyes luminous. She traced her finger over the nearest controls, her voice so soft he had to lean closer to hear the words. "I have enough deaths on my conscience."

"I told you before, none of this is your fault, starting with Sharmali's death on the first night." He admired her integrity, but was determined to keep her from shouldering the responsibility for things she couldn't have averted. "We never should have been here. *You* shouldn't have been here."

Squaring her shoulders, she met his gaze. "I appreciate what you're saying, but it was my fault once we landed. I was in charge."

Before she finished her sentence, he was hotly contesting her conclusion. "That incompetent screw-off Drewson was in charge. If he survived, which I doubt, he better hope I never cross his path."

"But I—"

"No, just no." He made a slashing motion with his hand. "I'm speaking from experience; don't carry the burden of what happened. Focus on the here and now, and us getting our remaining passengers—and ourselves—to safety. Once we've been extracted, once we're safe somewhere, you can go talk to the psychmeds. Hell, I'll go with you. The mind medicos'll help you see what I'm trying to tell you. Once we were put in this situation, did you and I do the best we could with what we knew and had available?"

Meg nodded, eyes wide.

"Yes, we did," he agreed with her conclusion. "And that's all we could have done. There are two people who would have died if we hadn't. Their lives are our comfort and our victory." He picked up the sandwich she'd made for him and took a bite, washing it down with the coffee. The strong emotions roiling his gut receded a bit. "Now, this is terrific. Where'd you find the coffee?"

"Someone's private stash." Meg strolled over to the other console, barely glanced at the readouts, and returned, as if she had excess energy she needed to work off. "Why are you so adamant about us getting rescued now?"

He swallowed another bite of the excellent sandwich. She might have concocted it from reconstituted dust, but right now it tasted better than the best Azrigone beef. Swirling the coffee in the blue glazed mug with the PolyStarMed logo, to savor the aroma, he said, "Remember the first time we talked about galactic war? When we were on the run from the Shemdylann?"

She nodded.

"We don't know our side is going to win this skirmish. We don't know they're even going to try. Strategy is calculated on a level so far beyond what you and I understand—Command and the Sectors' government play the entire game board, trying to beat the Mawreg once and for all someday. What if the decision is to abandon this system? The whole Sector?" He leaned closer to her. "What if the decision is to burn off this world? No one's going to care that we're here before turning on the torch. None of the four of us has the gravity to pull an external rescue on our own. The only reason I might have a chance is my contacts in Special Forces. And right now is the best time, while things are in flux out there, beyond this planet's atmosphere."

"I had no idea the situation was so dire." Meg sank onto the nearest chair, laying her head on the padded top, as if her knees had given way under the onslaught of his logic.

Guessing from her reaction, he'd painted the picture a bit too accurately; he tried to inject a hopeful note. "Max said he'd get back to me, so there might be a chance. He's a man of his word."

Raising her head and pushing her hair off her face, Meg asked, "An old comrade in arms, I take it?"

Red couldn't stop the grin, recalling old times. "Yeah, he was like my sixth brother. We survived Basic training together and then a lot of…really bad things. Too much action to talk about, outside the fence in a number of places, including Mawreg territory."

"But he's still on active duty?"

"Max was wired differently than me. He played politics, moved into the officer corps, and got promoted. I stayed on the Teams, doing missions. Until I couldn't anymore." As he drained the last drop from his mug, Red frowned. "Where exactly did you find this private stash of coffee?"

"On Level Two. We finished dinner and you were hard at work in here, so we forged ahead. There's a lot of personal stuff left, although a few of the rooms are stripped to the bare walls."

Anger mixed with concern for her safety burned through him. "I told you to wait for any more explorations until I was available."

Meg was unfazed, rising from her chair and shaking a finger at him. "And I'm in command, which you forget regularly." Giving him a small smile, she went on. "Callina was tired, falling asleep at the table. Her husband isn't in much better shape. I'm hoping he didn't break his ankle when he tripped getting in here today. It was bruising pretty spectacularly. Tomorrow we may have to see about activating the equipment in the sickbay." Eyes narrowed, she assessed him from head to toe. "You don't look too lively yourself."

"Plenty of fight left." Reaching out, he locked his hand around her wrist and drew her closer. He took it slow, in case she wasn't on board with what he had in mind.

Meg came willingly for a step or two, leaning her hip on the console and smiling at him. "Yeah, well, I decided the best course of action was to assign rooms for the night, and then check on you."

"Bringing me coffee and dinner. Which I appreciated."

"A good officer has to make sure her crew is well cared for." Her tone was low, teasing. She gestured at the now inactive panel. "Your friend's not calling again for twelve hours, right?"

"Affirmative." He rubbed the back of her hand with his thumb. "And I've set the monitors and alarms so no one can get near this place without us knowing."

"Even from above?"

Nodding, he agreed. "Definitely scanning for intruders from above."

"Well then, I think you need to have some rest."

A sense of duty drove him to admit, "I haven't checked out Level Four yet. I was about to run the scan when the first call came in from Max."

"I'm sure it's as abandoned as the rest of the place." She glanced at the bank of monitors. "And locked tight, so if something did happen on Four, it's been localized."

"I need to be sure."

She clucked her tongue, shaking her head. "Such devotion to duty. How long will the additional surveillance require?"

"Five minutes, maybe less."

"All right then. I'll be waiting for you on Level Two. I assigned us the largest room, first door to the left after exiting the gravlift."

"Us?" As he considered the ramifications of the room assignment, the blood pooled in his groin.

Meg blushed a little, but met his eyes. "Seemed to me we had a conversation to finish, some things to settle, maybe? I thought it would be nice to have privacy for wherever the discussion takes us. But if you don't like the idea, there are plenty of rooms; you can pick your own—"

Rising, he caught her to him, intending to savor a long kiss, his hands at her hips. She put her arms around his neck just as they bumped noses. Retreating a step, half smiling, she rubbed hers with the palm of her hand.

Frustrated beyond belief, he choked on his worry he was going to mess up yet again on impressing the one woman he really wanted to think the best of him. Feeling like the gawky boy he'd been on his first date, which further fueled his annoyance at himself, he tugged her close again, rubbing her nose with his in a caress as gentle as he could make it. "I'm sorry. I lose every ounce of self-possession when I'm near you. All the expensive military training the Sectors gave me, not to mention the discipline so painfully instilled, gone to waste."

"You don't have to try so hard," she whispered, tugging at his earlobe with her teeth. In between featherlight kisses along his jaw, she said, "I was never all that annoyed."

"You weren't?" He wrapped his arms around her, enjoying her soft curves pressed against his body. She was warm, smelling faintly of flowers and womanly mystery. His arousal grew even more urgent. "I believed you hated the deck I stumbled over."

She shook her head, the soft black curls tickling his throat. "Annoyance at your rookie screw-ups was fuel to keep myself from being too attracted." Raising her hazel eyes to look him full in the face, she said, "I guess I knew from the first day you came aboard the *Far Horizon* how special you were, could be, if I didn't keep my defenses solid. I didn't want to risk getting hurt again."

"I'd die before I hurt you."

"Sometimes it's not that easy to trust," she said, a flicker of strong emotion in her eyes.

He exhaled, instant anger at whoever had hurt her in the past rising to the top of his emotions. Realizing he couldn't defend her in the past, he compartmentalized the protective feelings. Trying for a lighter tone, he said, "Am I past the defenses now?"

For answer, she went on her tiptoes and kissed him. After the first moment when her soft lips rested against his, he tilted his head to get the right angle and let his tongue trace the contours, silently asking permission for entry. With a contented sigh, her body curving into his, she parted her lips slightly, her tongue touching his in undeniable invitation. Arms tightening to hold her closer, body suffused with pleasure, he deepened the caress, exploring the sensual pleasures of her mouth and tongue, tangling with her as he'd longed to do for weeks.

"Can't Level Four wait till tomorrow?" she asked when they parted, both panting a bit. "After all, it's been a couple of years since this place went on the inactive list."

He was tempted, but the blinking red indicators refused to be ignored. "Wait here with me then. I'll work faster with the visible incentive."

"Flatterer." She sank into the other chair, waving a languid hand for him to proceed.

But now Red encountered his first real roadblock since activating the control board. Level Four had extra layers of security applied. He tried the techniques which had gained him access to the other monitors and information, but nothing worked. "PolyStarMed made it a real challenge to see what's going on in Level Four, past or present." Frustrated, he banged his fist on the offending tab. "Sealed up tight, physically and visually."

"But there's no one down there, right?" Meg came to look over his shoulder.

He spun the chair to check the life support vitals. "Our party are the only living creatures registering in the entire facility." Pointing one hand at a line of sensors, he said, "Level Four does report here, to that extent."

"Well then, if you can't reconnoiter tonight, there's no use sitting here getting worked up over it. Maybe you can ask Bettis to help you tomorrow. He was pretty exhausted and in a lot of pain, but if you're worried, you could drag him up here now. Not sure how functional he'd be, though."

"Yeah, good idea to have Bettis take a look tomorrow, see if he can drill down further than I was able to." He stood, stretching. "I don't like not having complete intel on the situation around us—that kind of omission can bite you in the ass— but it seems we don't have any choice. No alarms sounding, no life forms down there on Four, guess I can wait a few more hours to check. We're not planning to live here long term anyway."

"So, you're ready to explore Level Two now?" Her voice was teasing, the sexual innuendo clear from her heavy lidded gaze.

"Only as far as the first door on the left, I think you said?"

Holding hands, Meg and Red strolled to the gravlift and made the short trip to the second level, stepping off into a reception area. Scanning his surroundings automatically, Red registered a built-in couch and several small tables, and hallways radiating off the main room.

Meg glanced at the closed doors on the first corridor. "Do you mind if I take a second to check on the Bettises?"

He craved her undivided attention for the rest of the night, but he could spare the brief time required to ease her concern about their passengers. "Of course not. Good idea, I'll come with you."

Meg walked softly across the floor and into the hall, Red on her heels. She knocked gently on the door, but got no answer. "I'm sure they're fine, probably asleep," Meg said, biting her lip. "I don't want to wake them." Her lips curved in a grin. "Or interrupt them, as the case may be. This is their honeymoon, after all."

"Callina's been a trooper. When we were on the beach, Finchon had a chance to ransom her along with his own sorry ass, and he refused." Red grew angry when he remembered the man's callousness.

"You're not serious?" Eyes wide, Meg stopped in her tracks.

"Apparently, there's no love lost between the two of them. We both know he could have ransomed all of us and not felt the effects on his credit account. I didn't expect him to pay for me, I don't mean comet dust to him, but I sure as hell expected him to save his stepdaughter and her husband at the very least. If I'd figured out a way to escape the cage before you arrived, I was going to take her with me. She was the weakest; she was my priority."

She cupped his cheek with one hand for a moment. "I know you'd never let them have Callina, not while you had breath left in your body."

He captured her hand and kissed her palm. "I'll try not to ever disappoint you, Meg, I swear. Soldier's oath."

"I don't think you could," she whispered. "Our room is this way."

CHAPTER SEVEN

Red allowed her to lead him to the room she'd picked for them. The Bettises had exchanged knowing glances when she staked a claim to it, but made no protest, only proceeded further along the hall and found another room with a large bed for themselves.

As soon as Meg crossed the threshold, Red on her heels, and the door closed behind him, he took her in his arms for another soul wrenching kiss, long and deep. He was an excellent kisser. His arousal made its presence known, hot and hard against her stomach where his body pressed close to hers. Suddenly impatient to see all of him, Meg wanted his clothes off *now*. Eyes closed, her tongue still busy tangling with his, she fumbled with the fastenings of his shirt. He tried to help and their hands bumped into each other. Breaking off the kiss with a laugh, he stood unmoving as she finished undoing the tabs, spreading the shirt open to reveal his muscular upper body and taut abs. She yanked the garment free of his pants and he shrugged it off.

She took a moment to admire the intricate dragon tattoo starting on his left shoulder, twining onto his back, where the unfurled wings followed the line of his shoulder blades. The tail extended the length of his spine and ended above his butt. The colors were intense—red and black, with hints of gold and turquoise. "This is amazing art." She traced the silhouette with a fingertip, feeling him shiver under her touch. The slight movement brought on an answering twinge deep in her. Her own arousal intensified. Free arm circling his waist, she pressed a kiss to the center of his back, rubbing her cheek against him. "I was watching from the trees when the Shemdylann examined this, when you were on the beach. I was terrified for you."

"Crxtahl asked me what it was and I told him some bullshit. Luckily, he believed me."

"Luckily? It's more than just a dragon?"

"It's the emblem of Team Twelve." She felt him squaring his shoulders as he spoke, unconsciously assuming a military stance. "If the enemy figured out I was Special Forces, I'd have had to obey Order One."

"I don't understand?" The mood had turned dark somehow. Puzzled, keeping her hand on him caressing his side and then the taut muscle of his abdomen, she moved to face him.

His face was set in grave lines, the usual cheerful expression gone. "We're not allowed to fall into enemy hands, Meg. We know too much, starting with the all access code. The code's the merest tip of the classified info in my head. Even if I am on inactive status, retired."

"But prisoners must get captured occasionally. How do you—"

"It's a Mellurean mind implant." He tapped his left temple. "Instant suicide."

Shocked, she leaned her head against him, wrapping her arms around his waist. The thought that she might have lost him was horrifying. "No."

"Has to be that way." She felt him shrug. The vibration of his deep voice rumbled against her ear as he continued. His strong arms held her tight. "You accept it or you aren't on the Teams. Simple decision, yes or no. Any good warrior makes peace with the idea of his death before he goes in harm's way."

"I had no idea." This stern military incarnation of the usually easygoing, cheerful Red was very different than anything she'd ever seen from him, almost like a stranger stood before her. But she'd grown up on the frontier; she was no sheltered Inner Sectors girl. This side of Red was reassuring to someone used to men of integrity and unyielding belief in doing what was right. She hadn't met many of those crewing luxury charter ships. If anything, his revelation strengthened her attraction to him. "My dad would have been happy if I'd brought you home. I'd be proud to introduce you."

Red hugged her. "I'm honored—I hope I get to meet him someday and tell him how special you are. But, hey, enough of this grim military talk. We get wide discretion on when to enact Order One. Obviously, since I'm still alive and kicking." He tilted her chin gently upward with one finger. "I give you my word of honor, I'll never abandon you." He kissed her lips and then asked, "My turn?" He gestured at her shirt.

With a little start, absorbed in thinking over what he'd revealed to her, she said, "Absolutely." She ran her hands over his chest, flicking the flat buttons of his nipples lightly, then sliding her palms down his body, skating her left under his waistband and inside his swim trunks. She grasped his heavy penis, delighted to find she couldn't quite circle his girth. Red took a deep breath as she stroked him, but continued to undo her shirt.

"A little help with this," he said, pulling on her sleeve.

Removing her hold, but not before a final caress across the top of his penis with her thumb, she shimmied and her uniform top fell to the floor on top of his. Meg thoroughly enjoyed his masculine murmur of approval as his hands went to the full cups of her black lace bra, tracing the lace with a fingertip, much as she'd admired his dragon tattoo. "Good thing I didn't know you had this confection on underneath that serious uniform. Gives me all kinds of ideas." He swallowed hard. "You're gorgeous," he said as he lowered his head to take her lips for another kiss.

His mouth was hot, coffee-flavored, his tongue tangling with hers possessively. Hard as it was to focus under the sensual attack, Meg persisted in her effort to undo the fastening of his trousers. Red stepped out of them and the swim trunks underneath as soon as she undid the belt and eased the garments off his hips. After kicking off his shoes, he picked her up and carried her to the bed, where he laid her on the mattress as gently as if she was a breakable piece of art. He stood by the bed for a moment, drinking her in with his eyes. The way he focused on her felt like a caress and she stretched like a cat, enjoying the moment.

A hot throbbing deep inside made Meg shift her hips as she gazed at his naked body, all muscles and hard planes, the jutting arousal leaving her in no doubt he found her as attractive. "Consider me impressed."

He laughed, eyes crinkling in that way she found so sexy every time he did it. Oh, yes, it had been hard to adhere to her self-imposed rule about no fraternization. "The feeling is mutual," he said, sitting at the end of the bed to remove her shoes, followed immediately by her slacks. He ran his hands up the outsides of her legs, pushing her thighs gently apart. Sliding a hand into the vee of her body, he shifted the gusset of her panties out of his way as he inserted two fingers into her. Leaning close, he whispered, "So hot and wet—your response to me turns me on like you wouldn't believe."

"We've been doing foreplay for quite a while now, haven't we?" she said, moving against him as he stroked his fingers in and out of her, massaging, testing what made her respond. He seemed to know all the right places to touch. Meg's arousal grew, the delicious tremors peaking under his attention.

"Ever since I signed onto the damn *Far Horizon*, and you started trying to ignore me." He slid her higher on the bed, then drew her underwear off ever so slowly before putting his mouth where his fingers had been, his tongue laving her sensitive places in a rhythm that had her threading her fingers in his hair, urging him on as the sensations built to an irresistible climax. She arched against him, holding him as close as she could, trying not to scream with pleasure as the orgasm unleashed in response to his caresses.

"You taste so good," he said, shifting to where he could gaze into her eyes. Slowly, he unfastened the bra, casting it aside on the floor. "The perfect size," he murmured, kneading her breasts with his hands for a moment before moving over her so he could swirl his tongue over first one nipple, then the other, tugging and sucking until she wanted to scream with pleasure.

Meg rubbed his shoulders and wrapped her legs around him, holding him as close as she possibly could. "I want you inside me."

"There's nothing I want more, but we don't have protection."

"We both had to give the captain clean health certificates from the Guild before we lifted off," she said. "So, I'm not worried. And I've had the injects, not getting pregnant this year."

"All right then, you don't have to invite me twice." As she parted her legs to give him access, he guided the blunt head of his penis into her soft folds.

Meg moaned in pleasure as his girth filled her, soothing the ache she'd had after her first orgasm, which had been intense, but nothing compared to what the more intimate contact would provide. As he pumped in and out, going slowly until she could get used to his size, she clenched her inner muscles in a rhythm she hoped would drive him to lose some control.

Red grunted and held still for a moment, buried deep inside her. Smoothing her hair from her face, he kissed her forehead. "I'm not going to last long if you keep doing that."

"We have all night, we can play this game more than once," she whispered.

"I like the way you think." He drew his hips back and then plunged into her, his release powerful, triggering her own as she fought to hold him as tightly as she could, locking her legs behind his butt to hold him. Losing track of where she ended and he began, Meg surrendered herself to the sensations deep in her core and splintered in a climax more intense than any she'd ever experienced before.

Hours later, there was a gentle knock on the door. A bit disoriented, lost in a good dream where she and Red were walking through shafts of sunlight in the woods on her home world, Meg didn't fully awaken until the second set of knocks. She rolled over, grabbing the sheet to cover herself and padded to the entry. Allowing the door to open a hand's width, not revealing the bed, she found Callina waiting. Brushing hair from her eyes, Meg said, "Did you sleep okay?"

"Yes, but now I'm hungry. Any problem with me going to Level One and finding myself some breakfast?"

"Sure, but stay away from the control room. Red has the sensors on and the communications alarms set. Is your husband awake yet?"

"No, he's finally getting some rest." Callina rubbed her eyes with one hand. "He was complaining about his ankle in the middle of the night."

"I'll examine it later," Red said from the bed.

Callina blushed a bit and her eyes widened at the sound of Red's voice. Giving Meg a wink, she said, "See you later then." With a wave of her hand, the woman headed for the gravlift.

Closing the portal, Meg turned to see Red watching her, his morning erection tenting the thin blanket in an invitation she had no intention of rejecting. She dropped the sheet, yanked the blanket away playfully, and climbed onto the bed, placing herself astride his thighs.

"Oh, like that is it?" Red said, shifting his hips to push his arousal against her.

"Like what?"

"Taking the command position?"

Meg rose slightly, caging him with one hand, guiding him into her. He thrust upward and she sank onto his shaft, wriggling a little.

He frowned. "Are you sure you're not too sore this morning?"

"Little late to be asking." She laughed and clenched her inner muscles massaging him the way she'd discovered drove him crazy, reaching to roll his balls between her fingers. "Although, I appreciate the concern."

Slowly he sat, raising himself with one arm behind him. Meg took her time moving until she was leaning on his thighs with her elbows. From that angle she was able to apply her own hip muscles to the task of intensifying their mutual pleasure. Brow furrowed, Red had a look of concentration on his face as he thrust, retreating slightly and plunging deeper on his next movement, Meg matching his every move from her position facing him. She hovered close to climax and apparently her partner did as well. "Don't worry, you won't hurt me," she said, taking a deep breath. Arching her spine she ground herself against him, her innermost muscles clenching in an orgasm that ignited his, finishing together. The sensations were as intoxicating as the first round of lovemaking, and the two delicious repeat performances since.

She moved to the side, Red's penis sliding from her body. He wrapped her in his arms and Meg could hear his heart beating a steady rhythm under her ear, the sound solid and reassuring. "I have a good feeling about today," she said, raising her head to gaze at him. "I think your friend is going to come through for us. I think the nightmare will end and we'll be safe. All of us."

Red kissed her forehead, holding her as if he'd never let go. "I hope you're right. I'm not going to relax until we're aboard some nice invincible battlecruiser, flying out of this part of the Sector."

"This room is equipped with an adequate refresher unit, by the way," she said. "Big enough for two."

"Woman, you're trying to kill me," he said with a laugh.

"Making up for lost time." She traced the dragon's neck as it curved over his shoulder. "You seemed to be on board with the program."

About an hour later, after a shower together turned major makeout session, finished off with more sex, Red taking her against the wall as the warm water cascaded over both their bodies like tropical rain, Meg got dressed.

"I wish we had fresh clothes," she said, wrinkling her nose as she buttoned her blouse.

"You said some of the quarters had things left in them?" He turned and eyed the storage compartment in the far wall. "Should we check?"

"I'm not too crazy about wearing someone else's clothes, but it would be nice to stop smelling like smoke and tree sap." Meg walked to the closet and opened the portal with a wave of her hand. The shelves were empty. She laughed. "Just our luck. Maybe I can find time today to search the other rooms."

"Later, I have to get to the com and see if Max calls." Red donned his uniform shirt.

"What if he doesn't? Will you call him again?"

Red shook his head. "Too risky. Too much chance the Shemdylann might detect the signal and investigate. We're on a twelve hour cycle now. If Max misses the first deadline, the next check-in time would be in twelve more hours."

She sat on the edge of the bed to fasten her shoes. "And if he doesn't?"

"I'll give him two cycles, assuming nothing else changes in our situation. But then I'd advise moving on if we don't hear otherwise. He wouldn't expect me to wait more than two days. We'd better go through this place top to bottom while we're killing time, figure out what to salvage, make some packs in case we're on the run again in a day or two." He grinned. "Take some clean shirts if there are any left here."

"Where would we go?" Meg stood, realizing she was sore in a few places, but discomfort was more than worth the pleasure Red had given her. The two of them fit together so well, in bed and out of it.

Rubbing his jaw, he said, "I'm going to search the installation databases today, see if there's any information on the planet's cave complexes or other geological formations we might use for permanent shelter."

She appreciated the way he always had a plan, or maybe even several. "What about the forest?"

He shook his head. "Not enough shelter from the storms. We were damn lucky I found the nest the second night or we might not have made it through the experience, weathering the forces of nature."

"You would have figured something out to save us." Meg put her arms around him, leaning her head on his chest. "You're a force of nature. In more ways than one."

Chuckling, he rubbed her lower back. "The forest was fine for a temporary refuge, but if we're going to have to live on Dantaralon, we need somewhere inconspicuous and permanent."

"Until someone burns off the entire planet."

He tilted her chin for a quick kiss. "Hey, I laid out the worst case scenario, which might never happen. Even the Shemdylann appear to value this world for its natural wonders."

"If I have to be marooned, I couldn't ask for a better companion than you."

"Likewise."

"We'd better get to Level One and keep the others from eating the storage pantry bare," she said.

When she arrived at the cafeteria a few moments later, her concern proved well founded. Several packages of the dried fruit and other delicacies lay open on the table. Callina was rummaging through the pantry, opening other containers to sniff and taste with careless disregard for the future.

Reasserting control, Meg walked along the line of storage compartments, closing each with a firm click. "We can eat whatever pleases us this morning to celebrate our safe arrival here, but after breakfast I'm making an inventory and we'll have to ration."

"Let's not open anything else," Red added.

Callina blinked. Setting down the container she'd been about to investigate, she cast a guilty look at the mess she'd made. "Oh, I didn't realize. I didn't think it mattered. We aren't going to be here long, are we?"

"The length of time remains to be seen. How's your husband's ankle?" Red asked.

"He's having trouble walking and it's all purple and black with bruises. That's why I came to this level alone to see what I could bring him to eat. Can you do anything for him?"

For all her carelessness, the woman did show genuine concern about her husband. Red left the kitchen to accompany her to Level Two to check on the man's condition.

Turning to see what she could throw together from the already unsealed packages, Meg pondered her emotions where Red was concerned. Starting the coffee brewing, she leaned on the counter for a moment, snacking on a reconstituted biscuit, wishing for some jam. She couldn't imagine her life going forward without Red at her side, so what was her hesitation? She'd certainly seen to the core of the man in the life and death situation they were in, and each new piece of knowledge about Red and who he was fit for her own nature and approach to life.

Were her previous bad experiences counting against him? "He's not anything like the men I met on my first crew." She said out loud. *He's the real deal and he's mine. I just have to say the word.*

Resolving to take the risk and tell him how much he meant to her the next time they were intimate, she poured the coffee as Red and the Bettises emerged from the gravlift.

She ran to help maneuver Mr. Bettis through the hall to the sickbay.

Eyeing the apparatus in the compact room, Red said, "I've had some training in first aid, but I'm no medic."

"Can you at least scan to see if the bone is broken?" Meg asked.

"No problem, I recognize the right equipment here. Let's get him on the table." Red started activating systems in the room, searching for the ones controlling the scanners. "Too bad there's no rejuve resonator in here—we could fix his ankle as good as new."

"Never mind those cost half the galaxy in credits and are for the military only," Meg said.

"Finchon has one at his main home, for his exclusive use. I'd settle for a major feelgood right now." Bettis clenched his jaw as his wife and Meg worked together to settle him on the padded examination table. "Make that three."

One of the circuits Red turned on activated the sealed cabinets. Meg searched through the shelves for injects. "Nothing," she reported. "Unlike the kitchen, the staff took the time to clear out all the actual meds."

"Anything we can use to splint this?" Red ran the scanning unit over Bettis's swollen, purple and black left ankle and checked the readout. "Good, not broken. A sprain."

"Are you sure? Hurts like the seven hells." Bettis lay motionless on the table's thin pad, clutching his wife's hand.

"The good news is sometimes it's hard to tell the difference between a sprain and a break, but the scanner's negative for bone damage. Bad news is soft tissue injuries can take longer to heal than breaks sometimes." Red took the sealed medical items from Meg. "Give me a few minutes and you'll be able to walk around more easily."

"As long as we don't have to go anywhere in a hurry, I'll be fine," their patient said.

Meg and Red exchanged glances over the table, but said nothing.

After breakfast, Red disappeared into the control chamber. Meg directed Callina on cleanup and together the women took inventory of the remaining foodstuffs. When they were done, tired of forcing herself to do her duty as the person in charge when she wanted to be elsewhere, Meg hastened to join Red.

She paused on the threshold. "It's almost time for Max to call in, isn't it?"

"Don't get your hopes too high, but yeah, we might hear from him any minute now." Red eyed the chrono built into the control unit. "If he calls, the signal will override anything else going on in here. No risk of missing the message."

Eyeing the red indicators for the sealed labs, she asked, "You still can't break into the security for scanning Level Four?"

"Haven't tried yet. I was accessing the databases relating to the planet's topography. Higher priority, in case we have to make another rapid departure. Found some likely cave formations about three hundred miles to the north of here. Of course at that latitude, we might get a bit too cold in the winter."

Meg shivered. "I hope we're not anywhere near this planet by the time winter sets in."

"You and me both. Nice enough place, but I never meant to stay here permanently. We could track south for better weather, but we'd have to make a long detour to avoid the Shemdylann at the Falls and I'd rather not be anywhere in their vicinity." Red tapped his finger on the applicable section of the readout on the large wall screen.

"Do you want me to go find Bettis, to work on unlocking the Level Four vids?"

Red shook his head. "We need to wait a few minutes. It's almost check in time for Max. And I don't want to talk to him in front of anyone other than you. The less anyone else knows about my military ties, the better."

"No argument from me. I guess since we've already been inside the building for so long, finding answers about the nature of the research can wait."

A loud pinging indicated an incoming message. Heart beating so fast dizziness threatened to overwhelm her, Meg leaned over the chair as Red activated the link. "Max, old buddy, what's the good word?"

"Don't talk, listen. You got one shot. Sending a robo in eighteen, keyed to your DNA, limited window. Get your party on board, fly it out of the atmosphere and hit hyperspace the moment you cross into clear space because the planet is surrounded by tangos, *crawling* with tangos, including the big guys, you get it?"

"Got it. Thanks, Max."

"Yeah, I'll take repayment in ten year old Suavarian whiskey, you're buying. Damn lucky for you I'm here on ops, and even luckier the Mellurean singled you out in front of the brass ten years ago. Apparently, her interest is noted in your official records with a red flag. Makes you special. Fly with the Lords of Space, Sergeant, 'cause there ain't no second chance this time."

The signal cut off.

Unsure exactly what had been arranged, Meg studied Red's face. "Why can't he send the ship now?"

Drumming his fingers on the console, he said, "You heard what he said about the enemy? The tangos?"

"Yes, not that I totally got it."

"We're not only in the middle of a Shemdylann nest, but Max was also telling me the Mawreg have moved in. I'm guessing the Sectors' military planners' assessment was our only chance is if the robo arrives in the dead of night, local time. Maybe there's something about the way the enemy fleet is positioned off-planet, I don't know. Point is, we can't miss that robo. Limited window means it'll self-destruct if I don't activate the controls within a certain amount of time." Anticipating the next question she was getting ready to ask, he said, "We don't let the enemy send our own ships back to us rigged as bombs or track them to the fleet's location. Max will have programmed the course into the AI for me."

"Okay, so we go outside and wait for the robo in the middle of the night." She shivered. "Lords of Space, I hope there won't be another storm. Bad weather must be our special curse."

"We don't go outside here," Red said. "This place sticks out like a sore thumb, especially since the idiots who built it cleared away a ring of the trees. And if the Shemdylann tracked us, they'll find this place, but maybe not the landing field. At least not right away. I'm starting to like PolyStarMed's decision to have the landing field a little removed."

"But the robo locks onto your DNA, if I understood Max? Landing where you are? Another military implant?"

"Yes, which I can't discuss. It'll land as close as its AI can get. I've got to go check out that tunnel and the landing field, see what we'll be facing tonight." Red stood, shoving the chair nearly to the wall. "I wish there'd been some weapons left in this place. Reconstituted delicacies and real coffee were nice, but an extra blaster or two would have been better. At last I was able to charge mine."

She laid a hand on his chest. "We should still find out about Level Four. I just have a bad feeling about why it's sealed off."

It took them some time to assist Bettis from the cafeteria into the control chamber. Callina trailed behind. Once the businessman was situated at a console off to the side of the room, he started playing with the keys, inputting commands and trying different paths. "The good news is that the limited AI here accepts my credentials." He grinned at Red. "Sometimes—not often enough—it pays to be Finchon's assistant." After a few minutes of intense concentration, he spun the chair around and gave them a thumbs up. "Okay, here goes, activating the cameras on the mysterious Level Four." He flipped a control and pressed a tab.

In the next moment, Meg stifled a scream and Red was cursing as the monitors showed them what was left of the fourth level. The entire lab area had been burned off, everything in front of them on the screens was black and twisted from the application of intense heat. Cages, half melted, were strewn among the debris. Eyes screwed shut, she swallowed hard, trying not to vomit. "Please tell me there aren't any bodies."

Red rested his hand on hers, squeezing. "I don't see any. What the seven hells kind of research did they do here?"

"I don't know, but obviously the management was pretty scared about anything getting loose." She opened her eyes and took one more swift glance at the scene. "Turn it off, please?"

Bettis complied and the room was silent for a long moment.

Red gave her a long hug. "I guess this explains why the place seemed to have been abandoned all of a sudden."

Lifting her head to meet his gaze, she said, "Yes, but we know someone retrieved a lot of the equipment later. I don't think terrified people fleeing in the middle of eating stopped to pack. Do you—do you think we're safe being here?"

He frowned. "For now. Whatever was in the Level Four lab must be contained or destroyed, or they would have taken out the entire facility."

"How do we know?" Realizing she was trembling, Meg clenched her fists and took some deep breaths.

"We don't," he admitted. "I'm guessing if PolyStarMed decontaminated Level Four so harshly, but left the place standing, the corporation was hoping to return and start research activities again."

Callina started to cry. "We're going to die from some horrible disease, aren't we?" Wide eyed, she stared from Red to Meg, apparently working herself into hysterics. "Why did you bring us here? Were you insane?"

"The crew is doing the best they can," her husband said, busily interfacing with the installation's limited AI. He seemed to Meg's eyes to be the most cheerful he'd been all during the charter and their time on the planet. "Why don't you go to the kitchen and make yourself something to calm your nerves, dear?"

Although she wanted to stay close to Red, especially now that she knew the truth about their temporary haven, Meg looped her arm over the distraught woman's shoulders and urged her out of the control room.

"My wife is kind of high strung," she heard Bettis say to Red as the door slid closed behind her.

No arguments there, pal. Meg wished there had been some feelgoods left in the sickbay. She might not be a medic, but even she could see Mrs. Bettis was a prime candidate for a couple of tranqs about now. Trying to imagine this passenger on a desperate, three hundred mile trek across Dantaralon, doomed to live in a cave for the rest of her life, Meg shook her head.

About an hour later, Red and Bettis appeared in the cafeteria, joined like they were in a three legged race, the latter man hopping on one foot.

"Got any real coffee left?" Red asked, as he helped the injured passenger into a chair.

Meg studied his face. "Bad news?"

"We should be okay." Leaning back in the chair, Red stretched and tried to smile, despite the tired lines etched beside his mouth. "Some ugly stuff it's just as well none of you had to watch."

"I'll second what he said." Bettis rubbed his forehead as if he had a headache. "Reading profit and loss statements and business intel is a lot easier."

"Hey, I'm glad you were able to access the right data," Red said. "I might or might not have been able to drill deep enough to find the details we needed. My access code is for physical doors and portals, not AI's."

Meg returned with coffee for Red and Bettis. She sat at the table as the two men took their mugs. "So, tell us?"

Red waved a hand. "You go ahead; you found it."

"Do we have anything to eat?" Bettis said. "Amazingly enough, I'm hungry. Something sweet, preferably."

Meg brought two packages of cookies. Callina snagged a plump, cake-y square dotted with bits of candy before Bettis could appropriate any. He swallowed his coffee and chewed a cookie, eyes closed. Brushing crumbs from his shirt, Bettis straightened. "Okay, PolyStarMed originally established this place to study the venom of the local fauna. One of the rangers wrote a scientific paper about the unusual lethality of pretty much all the indigenous species. After he retired, the ranger did a startup, hoping to use the venom as a template for new medical treatments. The company funded him, then bought his interest out when the decision was made to build this complex."

"By then, we think their research had turned to using the venoms as the basis for new weapons," Red said.

"It's only hinted at in the AI, but yeah, the experiments seem to have been designed more and more to explore that path." Bettis reached for another cookie. "The real fun commenced."

Not sure she heard right, Meg raised her hand. "Wait, weapons? For use against the Mawreg?"

Bettis shrugged. "By then, my boss was involved, and trust me, he makes it a corporate policy to sell to the highest bidder. But the venom wasn't the focus anymore."

"What was?" Meg liked this less and less.

"Pure happenstance, but the scientists had isolated a virus from one of the animals being studied. Unusually lethal. The researchers were trying to weaponize it on Level Four. And then one day, the bug got away from them. As best I could figure out, a lab animal bit a worker right through the protective suit. Messy and fatal." He swallowed hard, dropping the uneaten cookie on the table and wiping his fingers. "The last part of the history cache was pretty difficult to watch."

"Which is when the staff here evacuated," Red said. "We saw the footage from the monitors."

"So they burned out all of Level Four to sterilize it?" Meg asked, hoping PolyStarMed had done a thorough job.

"The building's AI took care of the task automatically and eliminated anything living on the level, down to the microbes," Red said. "If Level Four had been breached, the AI would have self-destructed the entire installation. No one would have survived. So I guess your caution was justified." He nodded at Meg.

Taking in the horror of the concept, she shivered. "I like this place less and less. Why didn't PolyStarMed start the research again, or return to it?"

Bettis held out his hands, palms up. "No idea. Maybe PolyStarMed lost their government funding. Once they'd cleared out, gone off-planet, it would have cost a lot to reinitiate the experiments. Finchon doesn't like projects that don't meet their goals on schedule. He shuts those down and moves on. PolyStarMed sent in a salvage team which, as we've seen, was slapdash about what to retrieve. End of story to date."

"So, to answer your concern," Red said to Meg. "There's no problem with us leaving here. No infection."

"As long as we don't go near Level Four, we should be fine." Bettis nodded.

"But surely the virus was eradicated when the AI incinerated the labs?" Meg asked.

"All indications I could find agree with your hopeful assessment." Bettis spun the cookie on the table.

"But?" Meg prompted.

"If we do anything causing the AI to believe Level Four has been breached, it torches the entire place, all the other Levels. I told you." Bettis rubbed his forehead again. "I'd like to go lie down, if you can help me to our room, Mr. Thomsill? My ankle hurts like it's on fire."

"No problem. Good idea for you to rest before we hike to the landing field in the middle of the night." Red circled the table to help Bettis stand and then supported him as the businessman limped toward the gravlift. He glanced at Meg over his shoulder. "I'll be right back and we can discuss next steps."

"Oh, and Callina? I got the AI set to play your favorite game," Bettis said to his wife. "You can log into it on any access panel."

She ran to give him a quick hug. "Thank you."

"Figured you might be getting bored."

Callina hastened across the cafeteria to a table with an AI interface, and a moment later the repetitive chiming music of a popular amusement sounded. "I'll make the volume quieter," she said, waving one hand in Meg's general direction.

"No worries. Enjoy." Meg gathered the cups and the cookies and headed to the kitchen area. "I'm ready to help you inventory or whatever it was you said we had to do," Callina called after her. "Just tell me when you need me."

Surprised she'd remembered, much less voluntarily showed up to help, Meg started opening cabinets. "No time like the present."

"The game can wait. Let me just finish this one challenge."

A moment later, she'd joined Meg in the kitchen. "Are we going to count every crumb and drop of juice in here?"

"We won't do it all right now, I promise. We'll get a good start and then take a break. I'm sure you'll want to check on your husband in a bit."

"Yes, thank you. We've only been married a short time and this was our honeymoon." Callina's cheeks were pink. "My stepfather wouldn't give Peter any time off, but he let me join the cruise."

"Generous." Meg couldn't keep the sarcasm out of her voice. She studied the shelf in front of her, deciding if the aracal nuts would be better to take, or the dried chivana. Probably both, for different reasons. She placed both packages on the counter behind her and moved on. "We did wonder about you."

"We?"

"The staff and stewardesses." Giving her a smile, Meg elaborated. "You didn't fit in with the other female guests."

"Finchon made a pass at me, once, right after we boarded the *Far Horizons*. He gave Peter some impossible assignment, data to research in case he could make a deal with Trever on the cruise. Then with my husband out of the way, he propositioned me. Said now that I was a grown woman, I reminded him of my mother. Swore that he'd never tell Peter if I agreed to sleep with him."

"Creepy." Meg shuddered.

"I never trusted him, even when I was a kid. I managed to get away, into the corridor and then some of the *Far Horizon* crew came along and he scuttled into his cabin. He didn't try again." Callina swallowed a sob. "I didn't tell Peter. I don't know why I'm telling you."

"Hey, no judgment from me. We take on cruise parties like Finchon's all the time. I've seen the entire spectrum of behavior, believe me."

"I suppose you must have." She took a handful of juice containers from Meg and carried them to the ever-growing stash on the far counter. "He's a nasty piece of work. When we were standing on the beach in front of those monsters and Cryxtahl said Finchon could ransom any or all of us, I thought we were saved.

And then he refused to help us. I'm sure it was his form of payback for my refusal to sleep with him."

Hearing the quaver in her companion's voice, Meg set the pack of biscuits she was holding on the counter and went to give Callina a hug. Patting her on the back, Meg said, "We're doing fine now, though. And once we get on that military shuttle tonight, we'll be free and clear, while Finchon probably has weeks left in the clutches of the Shemdylann before the ransom payment clears."

"I hope they torture him."

"Not likely, not when he's a big payday for them," Red said from the doorway. "They won't treat him with tenderness, though, if the idea is any consolation."

"I'll take what I can get." Callina moved away from Meg. "May I go to my husband now?" Not waiting for permission, she left, brushing past Red.

Meg met Red halfway, giving him a hug and lifting her face for what turned out to be a protracted kiss.

"I'm going to head out for the landing field," he said. "Gotta inspect the situation in the daylight, make plans for tonight."

"I'll go to Level Three with you."

"Good idea. You should be familiar with the tunnel."

She laughed, walking her fingers up the taut muscles of his stomach, and tweaking the tip of his nose. "I'll go to Level Three with you because now I'm over trying to hold you at arm's length, Mr. Thomsill, so I want to spend as much time with you as I can."

"And I'm most appreciative of the sentiment, believe me." Smiling, Red held her hand as they walked to retrieve the blaster from the charging station in the control room before retracing their steps to the gravlift.

"What would you have done if the cruise ended without us connecting?" she asked during the lazy descent. "If I'd managed to stay annoyed with you?"

"Laid in wait for you on the landing pad after the captain paid us off, and done my damnedest to convince you to give me a chance." Red glanced at her as he stopped their progress with one hand on the gravlift wall, the other round her wrist. "What would you have said?"

"Cruise over, no reason not to mingle. I hope I'd have been smart enough to say yes."

He drew her close. "No problem then. You're a smart lady, Miss Antille." He kissed her.

"Actually, I had a half-formed plan to waylay you and give you a chance to atone for all the rookie mistakes," she said, warmth blossoming in her cheeks as Red laughed, eyes sparkling in delighted surprise.

"Great minds work alike," he said. "But now isn't the time to explore the subject. Sadly. Sex in a gravlift can be interesting. Offers a lot of possibilities."

"I'm sure I wouldn't know," she said with a laugh.

He lifted his hand, allowing the gravlift to complete the final few feet of their commute to Level Three.

"Shouldn't you take someone with you out there to watch your six?" Meg asked when she stepped off in Level Three, following Red on his way to the service tunnel entrance.

"I'll be fine, used to working solo. Despite the name, we didn't go in as a team on every mission. I don't think the Bettises would be much use, and while I trust you to have my six—"

"I need to stay here and watch over them."

"Exactly."

Red showed her how to operate the air lock into the tunnel. "Just in case," he said.

"In case of what?"

Shifting his stance as if uncomfortable, he nevertheless met her eyes. "If you had to evacuate the installation and I'm not...not here. But only as a last resort."

"We'll be fine. There's been no sign of the pirates since the day you fooled their scanners with the tree dwellers. I'm sure the enemy has abandoned the fruitless chase and gone about their business by now." Meg tried to inject as much optimism in her voice as she could.

Red nodded, but didn't seem as convinced. "Promise me no one sets foot outside the building for any reason while I'm gone."

"Of course. Why do you even ask?"

"I trust you, but Callina can be pretty immature at times. I'm worried about her getting bored, which is why I asked Bettis to hook her up with some games.

The lovely Mrs. Bettis doesn't have any more survival instinct than those pretty, empty-headed birds she sang to the other day."

"I don't know, she told me she fended off a pass from Finchon. That took some instincts." Meg grinned. "What's going to happen to him?"

"The Shemdylann will ransom him, probably send him to Freemarket via a third party and then he can get home to the Sectors in style from there."

"No, I mean once he's home in the Sectors. Any punishment for not ransoming the rest of you? Letting people die on the beach?"

Frowning, Red traced the PolyStarMed emblem incised on the air lock door with one finger. "Generational billionaire. Probably has lawyers on staff who will fight the charges all the way to the Sectors Supreme Court for the next hundred years if anyone does try to nail him. We'll report, and we'll tell the truth, but don't expect much in the way of satisfying results. And, as Bettis was telling us earlier, Finchon's looped into the military R&D structure pretty tight. He'll probably get a slap on the wrist for doing a deal with the Shemdylann to save his ass."

"Him getting off so easily isn't fair."

Kissing her on the forehead, Red stepped across the threshold into the air lock. "I'm going to worry about getting us home safely, not Finchon, okay?"

"Why is there an air lock anyway? Same air in here as there is out there."

"In case anything escaped Level Four," Red reminded her.

Reluctantly, she activated the controls. "Don't take too long, okay?"

As the heavy door shut behind him, he waved a hand at her on the vidscreen, and turned to open the door leading into the tunnel.

Meg wished she'd asked him how long he was going to be gone. She sat with Callina for a while, playing the noisy colorful game, and she worked in the kitchen, sorting foodstuffs. She was in there when an alarm sounded. Heart pounding, Meg rushed from the kitchen as the klaxon cut off.

"Did you hear that?" Callina asked unnecessarily.

"I'd better get to the control room and see what happened."

The woman trailed her down the hall. "I hope the pirates aren't here."

"You and me both." Half formed plans cascaded through Meg's mind. Should she move the Bettises into the tunnel now? Move the food and water?

When she entered the control room, the situation seemed normal. Only a single indicator was glowing amber. Remembering from Red's tutorial earlier, the signal was connected to the aerial scanner, she hastened to the board and hit playback. Adrenaline pounding in her veins, she watched an unusual flitter pass over the installation, circling twice before flying off to the south.

"Did we see a Shemdylann ship?" Callina asked.

"Maybe. I never saw anything like it before." Meg sank into the chair, realizing her hands were trembling. "But it's gone now. Can you go ask your husband to join me here? I want him to check whether the entrance is securely locked. Tell him what happened."

Callina gave her a half salute and rushed off. Meg stayed in the chair, watching the overhead scanner, afraid of what she might see.

Moments later, Bettis hobbled in leaning on his wife and confirmed not only was the main entrance to the installation locked, the gravlift from the reception area to where they sat on Level One was also disabled, with the door sealed. "We'll be fine," he said, false cheer in his voice. "The Shemdylann might not even think it's worth their time to check this building. It looks pretty insignificant from above."

Meg and he sat together in the control room, eyeing the screens for what felt like hours. Mrs. Bettis said the waiting made her too tense, so she returned to the cafeteria.

"When is Thomsill getting back?" Bettis asked.

Jittery, Meg tried to keep her voice from shaking. "When he's done checking out the landing field."

"I wish we had some way to contact him, warn him." Bettis chewed his lip.

"Too risky to try the com link over there. The sound might attract the wrong attention. There's nothing he can do—" Meg broke off, gasping as the flyer appeared in the scanner again. "Lords of Space, it's landing."

The intruder was a small ship, and for a few moments after touching down in the grassy expanse, nothing happened. Then a ramp shot out and two hulking Shemdylann soldiers emerged, armed and cautious as they moved to the front portal.

"Turn off the alarms, will you?" Meg asked. "I can't think over the racket."

Bettis obliged her. "You do remember I, uh, can't move fast if we need to evacuate."

"You said the enemy couldn't get in."

He shook his head. "I said the door was locked."

"Will it withstand blaster fire?"

"I guess we're going to find out."

One of the soldiers raised his weapon and fired off a barrage of blue tinged energy at the entrance. He and his fellow leaped to opposite sides as the weapon's bolts rebounded from the material the PolyStarMed people had used to build the visible portion of their complex. A tree several hundred feet away cracked and toppled as the weapon's energy hit it. Tremors shook the earth around the building as the mighty tree, hundreds of feet tall, collapsed into the clear space, narrowly missing the entrance and the cowering soldiers.

"This would be funny if it were a trideo. Or if I wasn't actually here," Bettis said.

"Red wasn't kidding when he kept saying the Shemdylann weren't too bright."

"Well, not their workers and the lower ranks," Red said from the doorway. "The officers have smarts. The females are rumored to be the most intelligent, but have never been observed in the field. Intel suggests queens actually rule the homeworlds. The Shemdylann are a spacefaring race, after all, although we suspect the Mawreg gave them the technology, in return for doing their bidding." He came to stand beside Meg, resting a hand on her shoulder and bending over for a quick kiss. "How long has this been going on?"

"The ship flew overhead about half an hour ago, then returned, and the soldiers are trying the door." Meg's terror subsided a few notches with him standing reassuringly beside her. "How was the landing field?"

"Run down and overgrown, which is good for us. Nothing to cause the robo any problems."

"Maybe we should go out there now, wait there," Bettis said.

Red shook his head. "We're secure in here. If the enemy finds the landing pad and checks it out, their suspicions will be lulled if they don't find any signs of us.

Their scanners are capable of pinpointing our location if we're out in the open, remember?"

"Right." Bettis subsided into his chair, tapping the chrono with his fingertips. "Six hours standard to wait."

"Too long for me," Meg said. "We don't have any choice, do we?"

Red shook his head. "The extraction attempt will occur when Max said it would and not a moment earlier or later."

Meg had another discomfiting thought. "Is the tunnel mouth secure at the other end?"

"It opens in a small building that was damaged in a storm at some point. The access is locked tight, like the portals here." Red's answer was reassuring. "I'll take the watch if you want to start moving some supplies into the tunnel?"

"Why would she move anything?" Frowning, Bettis assessed them both, eyes bright with suspicion. "What do we need food and water for if we're leaving on a shuttle tonight?"

"Most likely we won't need anything," Meg said. "But if we miss the shuttle for any reason, Sectors' command won't send another. We want to be prepared."

"Then we come back here and sit it out," Bettis said. "The war has to end someday."

Surprised, Meg explained the logic. "Mr. Thomsill and I decided we'd be better off to move north and avoid all contact with the Shemdylann or any other enemy combatants."

"I'm not sure my wife and I would agree."

Red moved into the chair Meg had vacated. "That's your privilege. I'm not going to fight you over it. But Miss Antille and I'll be heading north without delay if the extraction fails. You're welcome to take your chances with us, or to stay here if you like the odds better." He shook his head at Meg when she opened her mouth to argue.

As she left the room, she decided Red was right. The Bettises were adults, and if the couple voted to stay here, even though the enemy plainly had the installation in their sights now, there was nothing she could do about it. But Red wouldn't let the planned escape into space fail, so worrying about what ifs was a waste of time. Squaring her shoulders, she headed for the kitchen and her stockpile.

Dinner in the cafeteria on Level One was tense. Red talked them through his plan for the night. "The tunnel has a few minor cave-ins along the way, nothing we can't get past, but the obstacles will slow us down." He glanced at Bettis. "And your ankle slows us even more, but it can't be helped. I have to be in place half an hour before the scheduled landing time, so the robo's AI can lock in on me the moment it breaks out of hyperspace above Dantaralon. It will track me if I have to shift positions, but we want a clean extract, in and out. So we'll leave here an hour ahead of time."

Meg opened her mouth to detail the items she and Callina had dragged into the tunnel, but was cut off by the alarms. "Lords of Space, now what?"

"We'd better go see." Red led the way to the control chamber, all four of them crowding inside.

The Shemdylann were back, in force. Three large flyers had landed in the artificial clearing in front of the entry. As Meg watched, heart pounding, soldiers exited from each and then Crxtahl appeared, Finchon walking beside him, still chained by the wrist, but appearing quite at ease, if a bit grubby and with a facial bruise or two. The two of them were talking as they approached the portal.

"Can we get sound?" Meg asked.

Red flipped a tab. "Old Ar-Taan-Crxtahl's lost a forelimb." He pointed at the screen. "See? He's regenerating. I'd guess he faced a few challenges over losing us. Just gonna make him more determined."

"They don't know we're here, though," Meg said, trying to reassure herself as much as the others.

Finchon's voice came through the audio. "Yes, this is the installation the crew was talking about evacuating to, the night before you arrived. The missing people will be here if they're anywhere on the planet."

"Son of a bitch, he's betraying us," Red swore.

There was a burst of speech in Shemdylann from the nearest soldiers.

"Telling the leader about their fruitless attempt to force the door," Red translated. "Saying we can't possibly be in here, because how would we gain entry when Shemdylann weapons couldn't breach the barrier. Not the best logic, so we'll see what their leader says."

"Maybe we'll be okay." Meg took a deep breath as Callina reached for her hand, squeezing tight.

The alien commander was not appeased by the protest from his soldier. He and his second in command approached the door, examining the portal closely, while their troops waited. The lower ranking officer crowded Crxtahl, uttering phrases in Shemdylann that Red merely said were veiled insults. "Preparatory to a challenge, if he doesn't gain access here, and fails again to recapture us."

The two Shemdylann faced off in front of the door, huge pincher claws opening and closing as the aliens sidled back and forth. Meg was reminded of poisonous insects as they postured. All that was missing were the stinger-barbed tails.

Yanking on the chain binding him, Finchon cleared his throat as both Shemdylann turned on him. "I can open it for you."

Meg couldn't believe her ears, but Finchon obligingly repeated himself, speaking louder.

Red swiveled to stare at Bettis. "Can he make good on his offer?"

Swallowing hard, Bettis said, "Yes. It's one of his idiosyncrasies. He has access to anything he owns, no matter how minor. He negotiates the stipulation into every contract and agreement. There's an entire programming section writing the necessary code. He likes to pay surprise visits to his minions sometimes."

"Why would he help them? He's going home as soon as the ransom's paid." Horror at the betrayal by Finchon made Meg nauseous.

"Maybe he doesn't want witnesses to what he did, especially his refusal to ransom my wife, his stepdaughter." Bettis pointed at Callina. "Maybe he's cut some new deal with the Shemdylann. That'd be like him." Bettis sounded admiring of his boss's penchant for negotiation.

"We move now," Red said. He grabbed Meg by the arm. "Don't stop for anything—run. Get to the tunnel and head for the landing field. Stay inside the tunnel for now. I'll catch up."

He was already pulling Bettis from the chair and half dragging the man into the corridor. "I'll get you to the gravlift and then you're on your own. Make the best time you can."

Callina ran ahead. Meg supported Mr. Bettis on the other side. When the four of them got to the gravlift, Red pushed their passenger into the beam and grabbed Meg for a fast kiss before urging her into the lift as well. He was right on her heels, drawing the blaster as he descended.

No stranger to antigrav, she twisted with one easy movement to face him. "What are you going to do? Why aren't you coming with us?"

"I'm going to take care of this problem once and for all. If I don't join you at the landing field by the pickup time, head north." Reaching Level Three, he hugged her close. "Promise me."

She clung to him, eyes wide and distressed. "You're scaring me."

"I'm going to breach Level Four and self-destruct this place, catch them in the blast, I hope. Otherwise, the enemy will follow us into the tunnel. Or there'll be some other nasty surprise from Finchon." He disentangled her hand from his. Giving her a gentle push into the antigrav stream, he said, "Now, go. We only have a few moments. Shemdylann can't handle antigrav, so that'll delay them a bit. Lucky for us, there's no other way to get into Level One."

Meg stepped onto the access pad for Level Three, but kept her hold on his shirt, tugging him nearer. "I love you, Simon Thomsill, so don't get yourself killed. That's an order."

"Yes, Ma'am." Leaning close to her, he lowered his voice and said, "I've been in love with you for weeks, you know." He kissed her cheek and pushed her through the open tunnel entrance, sealing the door with one rapid motion.

Meg watched through the portal for a moment as he dove into a rapid descent toward Level Four. Brushing the tears from her cheeks, she cycled the air lock and stepped into the tunnel to find the others waiting for her.

Red usually had no problem focusing on the mission imperative, but right now it was hard to clear his last glimpse of Meg from his mind. *Which could get us both killed. Concentrate, idiot.* Clenching the blaster in his fist, he arrowed to the Fourth Level. Red lights flashed and the large NO ACCESS sign on the exterior of the airlock drove home the fact this area of the complex had been a disaster area. Red hadn't told Meg, but seven researchers had been vaporized along with the lab animals and the virus in question. PolyStarMed hadn't been casual when they designed their precautions.

He wished he hadn't had to turn off the vid screens. He'd like to be able to see what Finchon and the Shemdylann were doing, whether they'd broken through from the reception level above ground to Level One yet. He didn't want the enemy to be able to see him, though. Hopefully, Finchon wasn't tech savvy enough to terminate the building's systems, and the pirates would have a hard time as well, unless someone on their team was a specialist in human tech.

At best, he probably had only a few minutes to get this job done. The building's AI had to be online for his plan to succeed and Shemdylann solutions to tech vexing or impeding them tended to be messy and large scale. Taking a deep breath, Red punched his access code into the Level Four air lock outer door.

He could hear sounds as the heavy portal cycled for opening, even as a robotic voice sounded a warning that he was about to access a restricted area. "As if I didn't already know where I was," he muttered, stepping from the entry area into the air lock. He didn't touch the controls to access the lab complex. Instead, he laid the blaster right next to the sealed inner door and set the weapon to overload. Fortunately, he'd been able to recharge the blaster to maximum on Level One. The blast wouldn't carry the explosive impact a military grade blaster could deliver, but he hoped it would be enough to convince the AI the Level had been successfully breached.

Backing onto the threshold, he assessed the blaster a final time as the weapon glowed red while the power core melted down. Cycling the air lock door to close, hoping to contain the blast and direct it more forcefully into Level Four, he leaped into the antigrav stream and kicked upward, like a waterdweller swimming against the current. He refused to think about the possibility of the antigrav being turned off while he was inside the tube, but it was with relief he landed on Level Three with both feet and caromed into the air lock.

It couldn't cycle fast enough for him and he was relieved Meg and the others had apparently heeded his orders and weren't waiting for him inside the tunnel. Breaking into a full out run, he headed away from the expected blast. The initial explosion, the blaster going critical, was a small vibration under his feet. Taking the warning, he dove over the first small cave-in, a pile of rocks and dirt oozing into the tunnel from the sidewall.

The earth shook. He heard the explosion and a loud metallic clang as the air lock door apparently blew into the tunnel. A long tongue of orange flame reached toward him as the AI responded to the "intrusion" into Level Four by incinerating the entire facility in a firestorm. Red buried his face in his arms and scrabbled as low as he could get behind the mound of dirt. As rapidly as it had expanded, the flame retreated, sucked into the research facility before it reached his position.

Ears ringing, he hoped the problems of Finchon and the Shemdylann commander's honor were now solved once and for all. Finchon had definitely put himself in the enemy camp by volunteering to open the above-ground entrance. Red had no regrets. Rising, he brushed himself off, turned on the hand lamp he'd brought, since the power was now gone, and trotted at a steady pace in the direction of the landing field.

All too soon, he rounded a gentle curve in the tunnel and came upon Meg and the others, examining a solid wall of debris from a cave-in, filling the entire tunnel. Aiming his hand lamp at the obstruction in front of her, frustration grated on his already tight nerves. So much for easy escapes. "What happened? Is everyone okay?"

Shining her light in his direction, angled so as not to blind him, Meg said, "Was that explosion you destroying the facility?"

"I encouraged the PolyStarMed AI to take the appropriate action." He eyed the pile of dirt and rocks beyond her, running his light over the barrier. "Well, we're not digging through this."

"You're calm about it." Bettis was slumped on the tunnel floor, leaning sideways against the wall. His wife hovered nearby.

"There's an access tunnel in the roof, about fifty feet behind us," Meg said before Red could get a word in edgewise.

Why was he even surprised she'd noticed the maintenance tunnel? Meg was always on top of things, which was part of what he loved about her. "Right. Time's wasting, we'd better get a move on." Helping Bettis to rise, Red followed Meg as she retreated from the cave-in to the spot where there was an access port in the ceiling. Smoke was drifting lazily through the tunnel in their direction and the air had an increasingly acrid tang. If the smaller vertical tunnel was compromised, their present position was a death trap.

Allowing Bettis to lean on the wall, Red moved underneath the access plate, the women on either side of him.

"Uncomfortably narrow," Meg said, eyeing the access door.

"But doable. The circumference has to be big enough for a guy or a robo, plus a toolkit. Can you climb on my shoulders and open the portal?" Red asked.

Meg nodded, divesting herself of the pack and handing her lamp to Callina. Red squatted so she could climb onto his broad shoulders, and then rose carefully to keep her balanced. She worked her way to a standing position and took her lamp back. Wrestling with the simple mechanism one-handed for a moment, Meg's efforts were rewarded as the manual control released the round cover with a loud click. She ducked as the cover fell open, dangling on its hinges, nearly hitting her.

Red caught her as if they'd practiced the maneuver.

"Thanks," she said. "Sorry, I should have known that would happen. Put me down and I'll get on your shoulders again."

Moments later, Red steadied her legs as Meg straightened to peer into the shaft.

"There's a ladder set into the wall," she said. "I can't see anything at the top, but I bet there's another cover." She glanced at him. "Shall I go ahead?"

"Yes. We'll follow."

Meg pulled herself into the tunnel and began climbing steadily.

Red made a stirrup with his hands. "Mrs. Bettis?"

Hands on her hips, she gave him a sour look. "What is it with you people and climbing?" As she stepped onto his clasped hands, she gave him a wink. "Promise me there won't be any more climbing in our future."

Red laughed. "The only thing you'll have to climb after this is the onramp to the shuttle; I swear."

Red lifted Callina, planning to boost her to the bottom of the ladder next. She grabbed his shirt, hands like claws, her grip was so tight. "Is my stepfather dead?"

"I don't know for sure, but probably." Red saw no point in sugarcoating the truth. If she was asking, she needed to know for a reason. "He was inside the building."

"Good. Then maybe I can stop having nightmares about him. He was cruel to people, animals, AI's—my Mom used to say she was sorry she married him. And then she died and left me alone with him. Mostly."

Red gave her a hug. "No more nightmares, okay?"

Callina nodded, lower lip caught between her teeth.

"Ready to climb?"

Nodding, she reached up with both hands, grabbing the first rung and beginning her ascent, as Red helped her balance. He watched her progress for a moment before he was satisfied she'd be fine. *Another candidate for the psychmeds to talk to, right along with Meg and me.*

Lowering his gaze, he found Bettis staring at him in the harsh glare of the lamp.

"Not sure I can do this with my ankle," Bettis said, coughing. "Maybe I should go last?"

"I appreciate the offer, but you sure as hell can't boost me. I probably outweigh you by a hundred pounds. And I'm a foot taller."

"How are you going to—?"

Red crouched and made a jump, hooking his fingers on the bottom rung, doing an easy chin up before he dropped to the tunnel floor. "We're wasting time. Use your arms to pull yourself up the ladder as much as you can. Push off each rung with your good foot. The air in here is getting dicey."

He got Bettis on his way and then repeated his jump, climbing as fast as he could behind the much slower businessman.

The climb was endless. Red calculated there was actually only about thirty feet between them and the surface, which he could have accomplished in no time. Bettis, however, moved slowly, taking long rest breaks. Word was shouted to them Meg had reached the top and successfully opened the hatch. On one level, he was relieved, but the opening at the top caused the tunnel to act like a chimney, drawing the noxious smoke and fumes from the burning installation to rush past him on its way to the sky. Lightheaded, Red gripped the rungs with a clenched hand as the available oxygen was replaced by toxins. He should have closed the lower hatch. It wasn't like him to make even a simple mistake. The fumes must be getting to him more than he'd realized. Well, he wasn't about to risk descending.

"You have to climb faster," he said to Bettis, hanging on the rungs above him. "We're going to suffocate in here."

"I'll make it. I can see the sky." Coughing, the businessman levered himself upward a few more feet. "She's his heir, you know."

"Callina?"

"Yes. It was part of his wife's prenup for the daughter to be named in his will. I find a certain irony in that, don't you?" Eyes gleaming, Bettis peered at him through the smoke. "His stepdaughter and I'll be running his business empire since he died on this backwater planet."

"I'll ponder irony later. Save your breath and *move.*" Red's wrist chrono had been stolen by the Shemdylann on the beach, but he had a refined sense of time. Worry gnawed at his nerves that the extraction shuttle might have already landed somewhere close by. If he was right, the clock was ticking on their chances of escape. The robo would only wait so long before self-destructing, if he didn't board and take control. Sure, he'd talked a good game to Meg about heading north and surviving off the land, but he wanted to take her home to the Sectors, where they both belonged, not revert to caveman status and die on Dantaralon.

Eventually, Bettis made it to the top and Red waited while Meg and Callina hauled the gasping man out of the tunnel, half dragging him into the grass. A few moments later, Red got himself out, turning to scan in the direction of the complex, even as he was pulling huge quantities of clean air into his lungs. Towering flames lit the night sky.

"Whatever the AI did set the nearby trees on fire," Meg said, hurrying to join him. "How can anything burn after the torrential rain the other night—?"

"As long as the fire distracts the Shemdylann." He wrapped his arms around her shoulders. "Are you okay?"

She leaned into him, her warm curves comforting against his body. "I'll be better when we see the shuttle land. How're you doing?"

"I'm good." He took in another lungful of clean night air. "Let's get our passengers to the landing field, shall we, Miss Antille?"

"Lead the way, Third Officer."

Using his handlamp judiciously, he took the lead, Meg bringing up the rear, and wove through the trees toward the landing field. The fugitives had to go to ground once when a pair of Shemdylann flitters raced overhead in the direction of the fire, but Red had the group on their feet and running a moment later, while he lagged behind with Bettis.

"Take point," he said to Meg. "I need to know if the shuttle is here yet."

All too soon, she came back. "The shuttle's already landed. At least I hope it's our shuttle. Definitely human, not Shemdylann. No sign of any activity."

"Lords of Space, I've got to get there before the AI runs out of time." He dropped Bettis to the grass as gently as he could and sprinted, ignoring the need for stealth or cover.

Meg was right, there was a small Special Forces shuttle parked on the landing field…nothing but a black silhouette, no lights. As he approached, he sent a silent thank you to Max for sending a top of the line flyer, fast and extremely difficult for the enemy to detect. This model even carried limited weaponry. He slammed his hand onto the access panel, allowing the AI to register his DNA signature. The hatch slid open, a ramp unfolding.

A moment later, Red was inside, making his way to the pilot's chair at the bow. "Sergeant Simon Thomsill, taking command of this vessel," he said formally as he sat.

"Acknowledged. "

A metal plate slid aside, revealing the instrument panel and controls. Luckily, the configuration on this model was close to ones he'd flown while on active duty.

"Enemy craft approaching from the west," the AI reported. "ETA two minutes."

"Begin engine sequence." Red ran to the door, cupping his hand to his mouth so his voice would carry as he yelled. "Hurry up, move it. We've got incoming."

He didn't dare step out of the shuttle to help, afraid the AI would interpret his absence in a negative manner.

Meg and Callina were half running, half dragging Bettis.

Red swore under his breath, wild with impatience to get the shuttle into the air. "We're sitting ducks here," he shouted to the two women.

Bettis collapsed short of the ramp, taking his wife with him, landing in a tangled heap. Meg kept her balance, pulling at both of them, trying to get one or the other to their feet.

Taking the risk of leaving the shuttle, Red covered the distance in a few steps, yanking Meg away from Callina and aiming her at their transport. "Seven hells, get inside."

He bent over the Bettises. "Go ahead, I'll carry him." As the wife hesitantly stepped onto the shuttle ramp, Red got the moaning man on his shoulders and carried him through the portal right on her heels. "Seal the ship!" he ordered the AI, dropping Bettis into a seat. "Lift off."

The AI obeyed, leaving the ground in a nearly vertical tilt. Red clawed at the seats as he worked his way to the controls. "Strap yourselves in," he yelled over his shoulder. "This is gonna be rough." He couldn't spare any time for his passengers. He had to get outside the atmosphere and make the jump to hyperdrive before any waiting Shemdylann or Mawreg got a tractor beam on them. Or blasted them from the sky. After struggling so hard to reach this point, Red wasn't prepared to be defeated now.

He wedged himself into the pilot's chair again and took the flight controls, jinking to the left as three Shemdylann fighters swooped in, trying to box the shuttle in and force it down. "More thrust!"

The AI obliged with a power boost, and the ship jumped even as it twisted and veered under Red's hands. "Fire at will," he said, knowing the AI was going to be better at targeting under these circumstances than he was. "How long till we reach hyperdrive threshold?" He spun the ship in another violent maneuver, then spun closer to the original course, hoping his passengers were securely in their seats.

"Two minutes, Sergeant." The AI's voice was calm.

He flew over and above the Shemdylann, realizing his ship was now close to the atmospheric boundary. He had to put a small amount of distance between himself and the planet, and he could order the ship to jump.

A Mawreg fighter cut across his bow and only adrenaline-fueled instant reflexes kept him from crashing into the enemy. Red spun his ship to the left and upward in a spiral, as the distance viewers showed him a massive Mawreg battleship sailing into view at the curve of the planet. A swarm of fighters was disgorging from its belly.

Two of the four moons shot past in the scanners, Red flying like a crazed comet and the AI firing the blasters, Shemdylann and Mawreg hot on their tail. "Hyperspace now," he said. "Now, dammit."

Thankfully, the AI was a military model and didn't argue with him about safety. The ship jolted as it entered hyperspace, all the monitors reflecting the intense blue light accompanying the move. "Course calculated."

Red took his hands off the controls. There was nothing else to be done. The AI would handle the docking with the military vessel dispatched to retrieve them. He half turned to leave the chair, but Meg was right there.

"The Bettises are okay, maybe shaken up a bit more, but nothing serious," she said. "Helluva flying job you did."

"We made it."

"Thanks to you," she said, swaying as their ship popped out of hyperspace close to a formation of imposing Sectors vessels.

The ship the AI headed for wasted no time in contacting them. "*Penelope* calling shuttle."

Red thumbed the tab. "All here and accounted for, *Penelope*. Thanks for the ride."

"Our pleasure, Sergeant," said the voice at the other end. "We'll bring you in on automatic. Any injuries? Do we need medics on the flight deck?"

"We're all a bit banged up, one bad ankle sprain, nothing serious." Red was occupied with drawing Meg into his lap, a process made difficult by the cramped quarters in the cockpit.

"We'll see you in five then. Oh, and Sergeant?"

Reluctantly, Red pulled back from the kiss he was enjoying. "Yeah?"

"Your cruise ship didn't make it, got blasted out of the sky before they could jump. The last civilian vessel out of the system before the enemy took control of the planetspace was the TDJ *Bluebird*. Our captain thought you'd want to know."

"Yeah, thanks."

Meg sat silently for a moment, her expression reflecting shock, as if she'd been punched in the gut. Red smoothed her hair off her face. "You okay?"

"It's hard to take in. I was so sure the *Far Horizon* must have escaped." She wiped away tears. "I hoped they had anyway."

He hugged her. "I'm sorry about your friends in the crew. I only worked with them a short time, but they seemed to be a good bunch of people."

"Yes, even Drewson had his good points. At times. None of them deserved to die in a war." She shivered as a new realization hit her. "If we'd gone with Drewson when he left Dantaralon, we'd have died too."

Red tilted her chin, searching her face. "Hey, it wasn't our time," he said. "We owe it to Drewson and all the others on the *Far Horizon* to make the best of the time we've been given."

She smiled at him. "Sounds poetic."

"See the effect you have on me?" He nuzzled her neck.

Peering at the huge ship looming ever larger in the monitors, she said, "You aren't conscripted to active duty now or something, are you?"

Raising his eyebrows and frowning, he said, "No, why?"

"The shuttle AI called you sergeant, and so did the com tech on the ship we're docking with."

"I'm guessing Max had to make a point of my rank as part of his sales job to get us an extraction mission. Trust me, the military does not want me. Command made their decision clear while I was fighting my separation orders." His face was stern, his eyes hooded.

An old wound, obviously. Meg rested her hand on his cheek. "Hey, remember me?"

Turning his head to kiss her palm, he said, "I've been waiting a long time to find you."

"So, what about that interview for a staff job on the CLC Line you promised me?" She grinned. "I might even break my rules about fraternizing with a fellow crew member."

"As long as it's this crew member," he said, pointing a finger at his chest.

"Who else would it be? Rules are highly overrated, I've decided." She lowered her head to brush his lips with hers. "I hope *Penelope* takes her time with the tractor beam."

"Military tends to be pretty efficient."

"Too bad." Meg sat straighter and smoothed her hair.

"I'll try to get us quarters together on the *Penelope*," he promised. "If I mention the Mellurean prophecy a few times, that ought to do the trick."

"What are the odds CLC would wait a little longer for you to report?" she asked, as there was a loud clang, signifying the shuttle was now inside the battleship and secure.

Head tilted, Red raised his eyebrows. "Maybe for a good enough reason. Why?"

"I'd like to take you home to meet my dad and my brothers. If you're not too intimidated by the idea?"

"After the Shemdylann, how bad can it be?" He laughed. "I'd face any challenge to please you."

"Likewise."

And the first Space Marines through the shuttle doorway cheered and applauded as Meg and Red kissed before leaving the cockpit hand in hand to welcome their rescuers.

***

Thank you for reading *Star Cruise: Marooned*! I hope you enjoyed it. If you did, please help other readers find this book:

1. This book is lendable, so send it to a friend who you think might like it so he or she can discover me, too.

2. Help other people find this book by writing a review.

3. Sign up for my new releases e-mail wordpress.us7.list-manage1.com/subs cribe?u=2a337b96e2ee1ee1250004b9d&id=7462393c9eso you can find out about the next book as soon as it's available.

4. Follow me on twitter @vscotttheauthor

5. Come like my Facebook page: www.facebook.com/pages/Veronica-Scott/177217415659637?ref=hl

ABOUT THE AUTHOR

Best Selling Science Fiction & Paranormal Romance author and "SciFi Encounters" columnist for the USA Today Happily Ever After blog, Veronica Scott grew up in a house with a library as its heart. Dad loved science fiction, Mom loved ancient history and Veronica thought there needed to be more romance in everything. When she ran out of books to read, she started writing her own stories.

Married young to her high school sweetheart then widowed, Veronica has two grown daughters, one grandson and cats Keanu and Jake.

Veronica's life has taken many twists and turns, but she always makes time to keep reading and writing. Everything is good source material for the next novel or the one after that, right? She's been through earthquakes, tornadoes and near death experiences…Always more stories to tell, new adventures to experience—Veronica's personal motto is, "Never boring."

Veronica is a three time winner of the SFR Galaxy Award and a National Excellence in Romance Fiction Award.

She's the proud recipient of a NASA Exceptional Service Medal but must hasten to add the honor was not for her romantic fiction!

Blog: http://veronicascott.wordpress.com/
Email: veronica.scott.author@gmail.com